I See Yellow Flowers in the Green Grass

Selected Short Stories, Books, Translations, and Adaptations
by Nguyễn Nhật Ánh

Cho tôi xin một vé đi tuổi thơ (*Ticket to Childhood*), translated
into English (2011), Korean (2013), Japanese (2020)

Mắt biếc (*Azure Eyes*), translated into Japanese (2004)

Đi qua hoa cúc (Say goodbye to the chrysanthemum flowers),
translated into Japanese (2020)

Kính Vạn Hoa (*Kaleidoscope*) (54 volumes)

Tôi là Bêtô (*I am Beto*)

Feature film of *I See Yellow Flowers in the Green Grass* by
Vietnamese American director Victor Vu (2015), with the title
Yellow Flowers on Green Grass

I See Yellow Flowers in the Green Grass

Nguyễn Nhật Ánh

Originally published in Vietnamese with the title
Tôi thấy hoa vàng trên cỏ xanh

Translated by Nhã Thuyên and Kaitlin Rees

Hannacroix Creek Books, Inc.
Stamford, Connecticut

Published in English throughout the world except in Vietnam (Tre
Publishing House, 2018) by:
Hannacroix Creek Books, Inc.
1127 High Ridge Road, #110
Stamford, Connecticut 06905 USA
e-mail: hannacroix@aol.com
website: https://wwww.hannacroixcreekbooks.com
Foreign rights inquiries to: hannacroix@aol.com

ISBN Number: 978-1-938998-86-7 (trade paperback)

Author's Note

I See Yellow Flowers in the Green Grass is a story of childhood in a poor village in central Vietnam, a childhood that belonged to this very author. When writing this story, it has been my hope that you, reader, will meet some part of your own childhood here too.

A college sophomore in Tokyo wrote to me after reading the Japanese translation of this story: "*I See Yellow Flowers in the Green Grass* stirs my nostalgia for innocent days. When I was little, I also used to play with a toad, just like Tường, but I no longer see those animals around my house anymore. People from the city often say, 'The countryside is so boring. There's nothing happening there.' But I don't think the same. There's so much in villages to learn about, as your book shows us. Thiều's village is full of beautiful landscapes, grasses and trees, wind, plus all kinds of insects. In Tokyo, such serene spaces are being lost, day by day. I have a great nostalgia for them."

I share this young woman's feeling, as I always acutely miss the absence of my own childhood. The world of childhood haunts me. I often ache for the old innocent days, often when I am aware of being so distant from them now. The only way I can possibly draw them back to me is to write. *I See Yellow Flowers in the Green Grass* is among my attempts to realize this desire. I hope you can meet your own childhood self in this book, even when the lives and habits of the kids in this book are not the same as yours. I believe that what belongs to the soul can be the same, whenever and wherever you are.

I only have the simple wish that this book can be a map for you. A map with which you can find some paths back to the treasure that you thought was forever lost: your own magical childhood.

I wish you a good trip.

Nguyễn Nhật Ánh

ngồi im trong gió nghe đêm rớt
chợt thấy hoa vàng trên cỏ xanh

sitting in wind with silent listening as night descends
the awe to see yellow flowers dotting the green grass

N.N.A

1.
fingers in bloom

Uncle Dan turns to me. "Open up your hand, my boy, let's have a look."

My fingers clench together and go into hiding behind my back. "But my hands are clean! I washed them just this morning."

Uncle Dan cracks into laughter. "I'm not planning an inspection. Just open up your hands and let's have a look to see how many fingers in bloom you have, that's all."

Behind my back, my two hands instantly relax. I extend the left one up to Uncle Dan's face, wondering, "So what's a finger in bloom anyway?"

Uncle Dan raises his eyebrows to look at me. "You're how old and you still don't know about fingers in bloom, eh?"

Taking hold of my hand, he explains so I can catch each word. "A finger is in bloom if the lines of your fingerprint form complete circles. The more fingers you have like this, the more beautiful your drawings are. If you have ten fingers in bloom, it means you can draw the most beautifully in your class. And write the most beautifully too."

1

My heart flutters as I watch Uncle Dan scrutinize each of my fingers. I feel like he's researching the veins of a leaf. Holding my breath, I ask, "So how many fingers in bloom do I have?"

Uncle Dan shakes his head, disappointed. "Not a single one."

I somberly repeat, "Not a single one."

Within that moment, I feel my eyes start to cloud. My heart gives a sharp squeeze and drops down to some place far away, perhaps to the tip of my toes.

"Don't worry, my boy!" Uncle Dan says as the glimmer in his eyes warms me up. "You're not left-handed, are you? The right hand, now that's the important one. Come on, pass your right hand over here!"

As if I've been fished out from underwater, I shove my right hand out and Uncle Dan carefully brings it up close to his eyes. This time his movements are extremely measured, as if he fears any sudden motion might distort my fingerprint form. As he's checking each fingertip for circles, he seems to grow more and more cautious, his lips pressing tensely and his eyebrows furrowing. I imagine he's observing little bugs through a magnifying glass.

"Ah, here we are!" he shouts in glee.

"A finger in bloom?!" The question bursts from my mouth, though I try to control the yelp and my stomach is in knots, fearing I've misheard.

"Yep, a finger in bloom!" Uncle Dan's face radiates like candles have just been lit in his eyes. "You have a blooming thumb."

My next question, "So, are there other fingers too?"

Uncle Dan clucks his tongue disapprovingly. "Patience!"

He tilts his head, gently grasping each finger with both his hands, mumbling under his breath, "Index finger, cripes,

2

defective! Middle finger, oh! How can there be nothing on this one either? Ah! Here we are, one more finger in bloom!"

I ask again, as if talking in my sleep, "Is it a finger in bloom?"

"Yeah, you dumb-dumb," Uncle Dan scolds me, though his eyes reveal their warmth. "That's what I'm looking for."

But that is the last blooming finger my uncle can find. The pinky on my right hand has nothing blooming at all. So altogether, two fingers with special talents: one thumb, one ring finger.

Uncle Dan then tells me to take a look at each finger-tip and begins a teacherly explanation. Just like he says, the lines forming the fingerprint of my left ring finger go in complete circles around one in the center, tiny like the kernel of a seed, and expand in larger ripples exactly like those I make when flinging pebbles into a pond. The blooming print on my thumb is not as even or as round, the lines swirl around with each other like a whirlpool. But Uncle Dan says it's still a finger in bloom—just that the thumb's bloom doesn't have the same beauty as some other kinds of flowers.

He looks out into the sunny yard, slightly narrowing his eyes. "Just look out into the yard and see. There are so many kinds of flowers, but they all don't have the same kind of beauty, right?"

Since that day, any time I meet someone I take their hand and ask to see if any of their fingers are in bloom.

My little brother Tường shockingly has six fingers in bloom.

"Oh, how can you have so many fingers in bloom like this?! You're going to grow up to write and draw so beautifully!"

"What's a finger in bloom?" Tường asks me, and I in turn give him the teacherly explanation.

His round eyes watch me. "And so how many fingers in bloom do you have then?"

I sigh. "Well, I've just got two of 'em." My voice is

heavy with disappointment, as if I were saying I only have two teeth or two toes.

Tường stands up on his tiptoes so he can put his arms around my shoulders. "But even so, I still can't draw as good as you. You're always the one who can draw the most beautifully."

Hearing him speak like this consoles me a bit.

At school, I take up my classmates' hands for close investigation. My heart sinks to realize that every other kid has more fingers in bloom than me. Especially my pal Little Plum: every single finger in bloom. Round swirls of fingerprints, all lined up one after the other. I look at her fingers' blossoming flowers, my voice green with envy. "You've really got a whole blooming hand here. I bet if your hands had six fingers like Old Mr. Five Bottles, you'd probably have twelve fingers in bloom."

Little Plum's neck reels. "Ew, no! I don't want twelve fingers in bloom at all!"

2.
the fingers

Since that day, I've taken to meditating on my two hands.

I'd never been much interested in them before, just directing the two hands to do this or that— take a note, sharpen a pencil, scratch my back, tussle with friends, tug Little Plum's hair, move a chair from here to there—and then usually just forgetting all about them.

But while sitting by myself, taking in the sun on the sidewalk, I have time now to admire my two hands. Have you ever admired your own hands? If you've ever done so, you'll see they're really quite nice.

You don't have to speak a word, just make a command

in your head, something like "Rise," and immediately your hands will obey. Both the right and left hands will rise if you want them both to. If you want them to clench into a fist, they'll clench. You can say "Everyone freeze! Only the thumb wiggle!" and the thumb will wiggle while the rest will stay there not daring to stir.

Your hands never resist you, that's why adults usually command their hands to do a lot of things, from good things like "hammer this nail" or "wash that shirt," to not at all good things like squeezing a trigger or setting off a bomb.

If you're a kid then surely you do like I sometimes do, which is command your hand to pick your nose or flick the ear of the girl who sits beside you in class, which are matters that my mom and teacher strictly forbid.

In general, our two hands are quite nice. They usually just quietly sit waiting for us to give an order. And yet we still never really show compassion to them, sometimes forcing them to do something dangerous enough to undergo a scratch or a lot of bleeding.

I love my two hands whenever I sit to admire them, which is usually after my mom finishes clipping my fingernails. That's when the fingers are like little kids who've just had a bath, all neat and cleanly cared for.

When scrutinizing my two fingers in bloom, on the thumb and ring finger of my right hand, I feel I really love these two fingers, even though there's not much to be proud of. It's like if you had ten children but only two of them were good in school, perhaps you'd swell with pride when talking with a neighbor lady: "Two of my little ones just got into college!" Or occasionally showing off a bit more: "Never seen the guys studying at all, but they still got into college, easy as pie!" Just to hear your neighbor gasp, "Oh, fiercely smart those two little fellas are!"

And as for the other fingers, I still love them. Actually I love them even more, the way that parents love their unlucky children. I bumble around some thoughts that later when I'm grown up, if I get married and have ten kids of my own, I will try to love those ten kids equally, though surely among the ten of them, the not-so-smart ones will be not as smart as the smart ones, and the not-so-cute ones will be not as cute as the cute ones, naturally.

Our hands are like two close friends, sharing all of life's joy and sadness with us. If you keep thinking about it you'll see that when you're bursting with excitement, the hands will vigorously clap into each other so as to double the joy in your heart. Or when you're crying, the hands will take turns steadily drying the tears that roll down your face. The hands will be like two fluttering birds that carefully brush away the glassy beads glistening on your face and bring you into the sun, wind, rain, to the freshness that puts the roses back in your cheeks.

Since this realization, I have the habit now of sticking my hands out the window beside my desk.

I bathe my hands in the rain until the fingertips wrinkle up and it's like the riddle we kids often say: *"What's a tree with five branches which withers when wet but without water stays fresh?"*

Then I fan them out like my mom hanging clothes to dry by the hedges so the fingers bask under sunlight, feeling the tickle of soft breeze.

Once Little Plum dropped by my house to play and saw me sticking my hands out the window, her eyes widening. "What's going on here?"

"I'm air drying my fingers, see. What, you've never air dried your fingers or something?"

"No."

"So when you get your hands wet, then what're you gonna do?"

"I just wipe them on my clothes."

I shrieked, "Aw ew, who wipes their hands on their clothes?"

A few days later I drop by Little Plum's house to buy some soy sauce (her family runs a grocery shop), and who do I see sitting there with hands sticking out the window exactly like mine? I ask, bubbling with pride, "Ah, so you're air drying your two hands here, huh?"

And she bubbles back to me, "Yeah! I just finished washing the dishes."

It wasn't so often that Little Plum would speak with such a cheerful voice like that.

"You're air drying your hands in some new other style then?" I ask one other time too, when seeing her hands against her chin, elbows resting on the windowsill, a dazed and distant look on her face.

"No. I'm not air drying my hands at all." Her voice dark and broken now, "I'm air drying my face."

"What happened to your face that you have to air dry it? You just took a bath or something?"

"No. My mom just beat me."

I don't ask anything else. I get it. Poor Little Plum, drying her teardrops.

3.
Uncle Dan

Uncle Dan's only older than me by eight years, the youngest of my dad's siblings. He lives with my grandma because he's the one child not yet married.

Because my grandma's house is not too far from mine, I usually pass by to see them there, and Uncle Dan usually passes by our house to see me and my brother.

Uncle Dan only has one arm. His right arm stops at the end of the elbow. Whenever he goes outside, one sleeve sways loose in the breeze like that of a scarecrow protecting the melons. But with the arm that's still there, he plays the harmonica, best in town.

My grandma says that Uncle Dan used to work with processing sugarcane. I have no idea how (he would probably have fallen asleep) but his arm got caught in the cane grinding machine, and it was broken and crushed. The doctor had to amputate it to save him.

That day he was looking at my fingers in bloom, I had forgotten to ask him how many he had, which troubled me for the rest of the day.

It was in the evening, just as I decided to pass by my grandma's house to go find my uncle, when I heard the noisy throat-clearing sounds at the top of the alley. To us kids, it's the signal that my uncle's coming, as if he's saying, "Hey Thiều, hey Tường! I'm here to play!"

I sprint out to the alley at the first sound of throat clearing.

"Hey, Uncle Dan! So how many fingers in bloom do you have?" I'm running and shouting at the same time.

"Me, eh?" He ruffles my hair with his only hand. "Before, I used to have five fingers in bloom. But now I don't have any at all."

"How's that?" I'm stupefied. "How'd the fingers in bloom disappear?"

"They didn't disappear!" Uncle Dan chuckles, dropping his hand from my head to stroke the stub of his arm. "It's just that all five of my fingers in bloom were on the right hand."

His right hand, of course, is the amputated one.

I say without thinking, "But even though your right hand isn't there anymore, you're still a person with five fingers in bloom, aren't you?"

He seems surprised by my logic. His eyes widen, staring at me as if seeing me for the first time. He looks like this without saying anything for long enough that it gives me the creeps.

"Did I say something wrong?"

"No! It's very interesting what you said! Such a simple thing that for so long I haven't realized. Hah! How terrific! Hey, everybody! I've still got five fingers in bloom!"

I confirm with my friends that Uncle Dan still has five fingers in bloom, it's just that no one can see them anymore. My uncle draws very beautifully. In Tường's eyes, I am the one who draws most beautifully. But in my eyes, it's Uncle Dan who's number one. For my drawing or writing exercises, when I'd rather be daydreaming I often go find my uncle to help me, and whenever I do, I get the highest marks in the class.

4.
Uncle Dan's ghost story

Since another lifetime ago, our house has sat beside a highway and behind it lies an immense cemetery. The cemetery is so vast that it even slips into our garden, and there are two deserted grave sites that have resided there since long before my family moved in.

Evenings at home, while watching the flickering sticks of incense that my mom lights before the graves every night, my brother and I feel, as any kid would, a kind of spookiness.

And so it is that whenever Uncle Dan comes over, he gathers my brother and me to listen to his ghost stories.

Though Uncle Dan is an excellent harmonica player, he seems to have no interest in performing for us. Beg him to play, he'll take the little instrument out of his pocket, surf it gently across his lips, come up with some short-lived melodies, then stuff it back into his pocket saying, "Out of breath already," with the look of someone who's just eaten rotten corn.

Uncle Dan says he is out of breath but then keeps talking—"Let me tell you guys a ghost story"—at which point I know he's not even close to being out of breath. Uncle Dan can talk the ears off a wooden horse, finishing one story just to begin another. And all of them are such grisly tales, how he knows them so well is beyond me.

We sit with ears perked, silent with anticipation and fear, every now and then glancing at the door, hearts pounding, catching the flickering light from the two graves in the corner of the garden.

Uncle Dan tells the story of Lady Thoan, who goes to collect firewood in the forest and runs into a ghost who disappears her for two whole days in the woods. Going out to search by lantern light, eventually her family finds her passed out , unconscious from hunger and cold. After she's back home, her belly starts to grow a lump. Her mother and grandmother suspect a romantic affair. But despite all their interrogating, she keeps denying it, which ignites their anger. They beat the living daylight out of her and back into her, then cruelly hide her in the shed. Nine months later she gives birth to a bundle of clothing and everyone realizes she's been cursed.

Uncle Dan then tells the story of a guy named Chair who goes out to farm and when coming back home at high noon meets his father, Old Mr. Five Bottles, on the way. Chair says, "Where you going, Pops?" But when back home he sees his dad sitting and playing chess as usual with Mr. Bé, their neighbor. Upon asking, he learns his dad has been playing chess since morning. Chair then falls gravely ill and is sick for a whole month, verging on death while also suffering his dad's reprimands.

"How could you be so stupid? The noontime hour of the horse is when the ghosts are out. If you randomly run into anyone or randomly hear anyone calling you, you don't make a sound. But you, you met a ghost and opened your mouth to say something. If not for the grace of our ancestors you'd have gotten your soul sucked away."

Of all Uncle Dan's ghost stories, though, the one I like most is the story of Old Man Huấn's house.

Old Man Huấn has the only two-story house in town and a ghost has been occupying it since the time of its previous owner, though Old Man Huấn doesn't know. The ground floor has a lofted space where his son, Sơn, sleeps. Sơn usually sleeps in just a tank top, always removing his button-down shirt and hanging it on a hook before lying down. One morning, Sơn wakes up and reaches for his shirt only to realize that the white shirt has turned pink. He feels around inside it and his hand encounters something wet. Bringing the shirt into the light for closer inspection, he sees it is soaked in blood, and a panicked shrieking pours out of him. He frantically chucks the shirt to the ground and runs away.

Old Man Huấn invites a clairvoyant medium over to the house. The medium spends three days scouring the entire house then declares that there's a ghost among them.. Old Man Huấn asks, "How did my son's shirt get bloody?"

"That was from the middle of the night when the ghost put on his shirt for fun." The medium continues, "Have you recently had any food go bad?"

Old Mrs. Huấn turns her head. "How did you know?"

The medium shrugs his shoulders. "How could I not know? Food spoils when a ghost touches it."

The next day Old Man Huấn, with an umbrella in arm, takes a bus into town to look for the former owner of the house.

When he returns his wife asks, "So what happened?"

He replies gravely, "He confirmed it: his daughter took a gambler for a husband and after the guy went to prison, the girl hung herself upstairs in grief."

Old Mr. Huấn later recounts this to the medium, who then climbs back up into the loft and gropes along the walls until he finds a rectangular molding.

"Here is where a window used to be that someone caulked over," he explains. "There's a Buddhist altar upstairs and the ghost doesn't dare stay there, so it comes down into the house. When the last owner caulked over the window in here, the ghost got stuck."

Old Man Huấn's face pales. "So what do we do?"

The medium says, "Carve out the wall so the ghost can slip out. Afterwards you can caulk it back up again."

I ask Uncle Dan, "But how to know if the ghost slips out or not, if no one can see her?"

Uncle Dan narrows his gaze at me. "The eyes of normal people can't see ghosts, but a clairvoyant's eyes can see them very well."

Little Tường is confident. "The ghost won't dare slip out."

"Why?" I ask.

Tường says, "She's afraid of the Buddhas upstairs."

Uncle Dan pushes back, "You silly, the ghost won't live upstairs. She'll only go up there to bow before the Buddhas, that's all, and after that she'll get reincarnated into another life."

But the guy Tường doesn't let up. He is always asking the basic, tired old question, "Why can't the ghost slip out through the front door?"

Uncle Dan replies with his basic, tired old answer, "Ghosts never go out the front door. They only go out through the back door or the side door."

And that's the whole ghost story of Old Man Huấn's house, but my brother and I really like it. Whenever hearing this story, I envision the scene: a ghost picks up Sơn's shirt and tries it on, and when it comes off all bloodied, I feel my belly twist up like someone's tied it in a knot. I also like to imagine the scene of the ghost cooped up in the house, just like a little kid, surely crying but with no one in Old Man Huấn's house who can hear.

Tường and I like this story so much that whenever Uncle Dan dives into telling of Lady Thoan or the guy Chair, we go a little nuts. "Tell the one of Old Man Huấn's house!"

"Tell how his son, Sơn, chucks the shirt then runs away."

This is Uncle Dan's way of being with us. He rolls up the sleeve of his missing arm, tries to arrange his posture neatly, then clears his throat with a stifled laugh.

"Old Man Huấn has the only two-story house in town, with a ghost who's been there since the last owner . . ."

At such times, waiting for the story, my brother and I instinctively scoot closer, our jaw is dropped and hair is made to stand on end, delighted and terrified.

To sink us deeper in our fear, when finishing the story Uncle Dan scans the room with his eyes and softly screeches, "Oh! Ghost! Ghost! Over there!"

As always when Uncle Dan spooks us, we are speechless for a moment before suddenly erupting in screams, shooting out of our chairs as if we were launched from a seesaw, and running loose in wild fear.

Hearing our fearful shrieking, my dad charges downstairs. He stands in the middle of my frantic path to block me and grabs me by the neck. "What's going on, son?"

With the blood drained from my face, I can only point to Uncle Dan in his shrill laughter and manage to stammer, "Uncle Dan spooked us."

My dad snatches the bamboo cane used for training dogs that's resting against the wall and turns to my uncle. "I oughta crack some sense into you, Dan. A grown man still playing such stupid games!"

Uncle Dan darts into the shadows, quick as lightning. Gripping the cane my dad chases after him. Not knowing if the cane ever meets its target, I just listen to the thudding steps of two brothers chasing each other down the sidewalk.

After running for a while, Uncle Dan swings out of our gate and stumbles onto the highway to speed back to Grandma's house. Disgruntled, my dad comes back huffing and puffing.

For the whole of my childhood, Uncle Dan's ghost stories will conclude with this little number. The chasing episodes between my dad and uncle only end the day that Uncle Dan silently leaves town in search of Sister Vinh.

5.

my dad's cane

There's a cane resting against the wall that my dad usually brings along when going out at night so he can fend off angry dogs.

I don't know if he's ever struck any dog that rushes up to his leg, just like I don't know if he's ever successfully struck my Uncle Dan's body.

But so many times that cane has beat my own back and behind.

My dad's a talker. He'll usually bring me somewhere to play and no matter where we go, people are drawn into and dazzled by his stories. Every time he tells the story of the famous figures Xue Dingshan or Zhong Wu Yen, people gravitate to him by the dozens to listen, their faces transfixed into stone as if their souls were sucked out.

Dad's also got a talent for reciting poetry.

In town there's a man called Mr. Four Cang who has lived just with his daughter, Little Three, ever since his wife died. Four Cang raises two buffaloes who always wear bells around their necks so whenever they stray, he can track them by their jingling sound. Wherever his two buffaloes go, the kids will gather around. When you hear the bells, you imagine the ice cream truck is going by, so people in town call him "Old Man Ice Cream."

Four Cang and his daughter work as day laborers in the fields. One day, the two are toiling away with the rice harvest and they cut into a patch of the paddy that's home to sawflies. Little Three gets stung in her butt and cries out. Four Cang bursts into worry—"What happened, child? What happened?"—and a flock of sawflies swarms around, stinging him right in the groin. He throws off the scythe that he is working with and sprints along a stretch of the field. He runs for some distance and then checks his groin, yelping to the high heavens.

My dad recites a poem to tease him, and now the cow herding kids repeat it everywhere they go:

A bee stings Little Three / Then turns to sting Old Man Ice Cream / The old man checks his groin with care / Two balls plus one more there.

Though my dad's just playing around, Four Cang takes his machete and trails him for a whole week.

Or the story about when the First Mr. Hớn won the lottery. His entire life, the First Mr. Hớn only bought a single lottery ticket, and thinking he'd never win, he took some cooling rice and stuck the ticket to a pillar in the middle of the house for decoration. Against all odds, the First Mr. Hớn in fact had a winning ticket for the highest prize.

The First Mr. Hớn was overjoyed when he found out, but could do nothing to unstick the lottery ticket from the pillar. Afraid that trying to peel it off would rip it, he sawed apart the pillar of the house and carried it on his back down to the highway to take a bus into the city and collect his winnings. In the end, the First Mr. Hớn was able to collect his money but on the way, while carrying the pillar on his shoulders, he knocked down a dozen or so people. Though no one was killed, the money needed to compensate those injured for their medical costs or hospital stays nearly totaled the amount he won in the lottery. And, without a central pillar in the house, his roof started to sag lower and lower until some days later a big rain came and nearly caved the whole thing in. His family quickly made a run for it to escape, but the next day the First Mr. Hớn needed to go around taking loans out everywhere to be able to rebuild the house. His mouth now twists to the side as if having suffered a stroke.

My dad, of course, was immediately on the scene with a line:

The lottery brings bombs / The one who hugs a pillar now hugs his debt.

When the kids teasingly sing the lines one day, the First Mr. Hớn promptly comes over to the house looking for my dad. He comes empty-handed, just to lay his emotions bare.

"You're right, it's like my house has been bombed. Would you kindly lend me a bit?"

When out, my dad is good natured and pleasant, but upon returning home he is often bitterly mean. My brother and I regularly take beatings. My dad doesn't know where to store the rattan switch, so he keeps it hanging on the wall. Each time my brother and I make any mistake, he presses his lips together and takes out the switch, first "to scratch" and then "to smack." I've been beaten to the point that I soiled my pants from the pain, and had horizontal and vertical welts covering my body.

My mom gets really scared when this happens, and one time she secretly took the switch from the wall and hid it. When in a rage and not able to find the switch, my dad grabbed the cane for hitting dogs and cracked it against my back.

So then my mom secretly put the switch back in its old spot.

Ever since, my brother and I get beaten with canes and switches both.

6.
Little Plum's house

Every kid has hundreds of reasons, hundreds of faults, to take a beating for.

The biggest of my faults is being afraid of ghosts.

With this fear, I don't dare to go through the cemetery by night, though by day it's a wonderful field for us kids to play in. I follow my cowboy friends, leaping over the mounds, frolicking around with games of play capture and tag, and then always flying kites at the end, everyone's favorite. Pulling a paper kite against the wind, blissfully watching it soar, letting out more and more line—it all gives me the feeling that I'm holding up the whole sky with my hands. I let out the whole of the line then fasten the end to the willow tree's trunk. Then, resting my head on a log, I face the blue sphere above and admire the kite's gliding wings.

But when night pours down its patches of darkness, the world around me suddenly wears a different face. Fireflies flicker among the night cemetery's will-o'-the-wisps, and whenever I have to pass by, the hairs on the back of my neck rise. Uncle Dan's ghost stories play out one by one across my mind until I'm on the verge of fainting.

Little Plum's family's grocery store is a bit far from my house. My mom often sends me there to buy things—sometimes duck eggs, sometimes a bottle of fish sauce—often when it's completely dark outside, which is pure torture to me.

This year I'm in seventh grade, thirteen years old and still afraid of ghosts. With dread, I pass the cemetery under the hazy light of stars, a shadowy feeling that someone's behind me. When turning around to look, I see no one. But just as I turn back and keep walking, I hear the footsteps directly behind me. Frightened out of my mind, I take off running and whoever's behind me also starts running. The pounding steps in my ears make me nearly crap my pants. It's always like this. When I finally pop my head into the shop, surprised Little Plum asks, "Why do you look like the devil's been at your tail, Thiều?" I refuse to admit I'm afraid of ghosts. I say I was just chased by some dog. I can tell by her face that she doesn't believe me, but she doesn't say so. My house is connected to her house by the cemetery. There isn't anything else in between us so there's no other possible dog it could be besides her Vện.

Vện is Plum's family dog and very old. Its eyes are nearly blind and its ears and nose are no longer very sensitive either, but of course the dog can still notice when I enter the house. It lies quietly under the bed, turns its butt in my direction, and lazily wags its tail to say hi.

Vện is exactly like its owner, Little Plum's dad. Little Plum's dad also lost his vision, from cataracts, I heard my dad say. When his eyes were still good, he worked as a hairdresser. He was one of only two hairdressers in the village, and while the other hairdresser wandered from place to place, Little Plum's dad was cooler because he worked from his own house, hanging a cardboard sign on the front door with the words HAIR STYLE scribbled on it. I got my haircuts from Little Plum's dad for a long time.

But my father eventually stopped letting me go to Plum's dad for my haircuts. One time, he almost cut off someone's ear, another time he made someone's chin bleed. Then one day our neighbor saw a red irritation on his skin, which, about half a month later, was joined by some white flecks. He would scratch at his skin while cutting hair and when he scratched, the white flakes would peel off and scatter like white chalk powder. People said he had leprosy. And someone said it was the leprosy that caused his blindness. There were no sure facts about that, but his customers gradually dwindled.

It wasn't much later that the hair salon had to close. Little Plum and her mom opened the grocery shop to get by day to day.

Every evening this scene repeats: I take the duck eggs or the bottle of fish sauce from Little Plum's hands and zip out of there as fast as I can, sprinting in terror all the way home with my two eyes nearly shut so my gaze won't be drawn to the cemetery. So many times I trip on the road, so many times the things I'm carrying break, and when I'm back home, if the egg whites and yolks are not dripping all over my body, then there will be a strong smell of fish sauce on my hands.

If my dad sees it, he beats my back with the cane. My mom warns, "Please stop it, dear, he's just scared of ghosts." But my dad keeps smacking the cane even more cruelly against my body and growls, "Ghosts? Ghosts in your eyes! At this age still scared of ghosts, huh?!"

Then my back is covered in welts.

Then at night my mother is crying as she wipes clean the wounds.

7.
the guy Tường

As it happens throughout our childhood, it's not me who's beaten as much as it is Tường, my little brother.

Tường is quite a handsome kid, a beauty from the very beginning. He inherited the lovely slender face of our mom, and the big eyes with long eyelashes of my dad. He's got thick, silky hair and rosy skin, his mouth wide with teeth that are straight and white like rows of carefully arranged and polished pebbles. Whenever Tường smiles, his face just glows. That beautiful angelic face and smile seem to bring an inexplicable happiness to those around him.

But between us, he's the one who gets the most beatings from my dad, not because he's naughty but because he has a sly older brother.

One time, I lure him away from the noontime nap and we escape over to the empty grounds near our house to throw stones.

The village is planning to build a public clinic on these grounds. The gravel is piled up and ready, but without enough money to realize the project, the piles just sit there. The gravel stones are small but hard as steel, all edges sharp as knives. They can split your head if someone throws one at you, which is why Tường is so scared.

He looks stunned before the pile of stones, his neck coiling back into his body.

"I don't wanna play. I catch a stone in the head and I'm dead."

"What are you talking about?!" I try to calm him. "We'll stand a big distance apart and throw stones at each other, and when you see the stone flying toward you, jump away. If we stand far enough apart, even if we get hit by the stones, they're not gonna hurt."

Tường doesn't seem convinced. He looks at the blazing red of the flame tree across the road.

"Or we could pluck the seed bones from those flowers and have chicken fights?"

The flame tree bears flowers with a "seed bone" pistil that is long and thin with a brown, rice-shaped head. Us kids often play a chicken fighting game with these pistils where we take two pistils as the "chickens" whose heads we hook together and then yank back. Whichever one's head pops off is the loser. In summer, I often play this game with red flowers, but now I'm more interested in throwing stones.

My lip curls. "Such a girly game. We're boys. Boys should play with stones or knives." I peek at Tường from the corner of my eye and say with some calculation, "Or you just want to throw knives instead, eh?"

When hearing "throw knives," Tường shudders in fear. "Ok, let's throw stones then!"

As soon as the words leave his mouth, he bolts to the edge of the main road and turns his head back in a frenzy. "I'll stand here, that's ok?"

"Ok, you stand there. Start throwing!"

I bend down to pick up two stones, one for each hand.

Tường clumsily clutches stones in his hands too.

I stand at the edge of the cemetery, Tường stands over by the main road, and we start hurling gravel stones at each other. For a whole hour, a rain of stones falls down on the radiant afternoon, glistening in the sun and whizzing through the air.

Tường is a better thrower than me. The stones soar from his hands and land quickly, precisely.

The more I play, the more frustrated I get: dozens of times Tường's stones meet their target. The stones fly through the air and even if they just graze my body and don't hurt so much, they still drive me crazy. The worst thing is that I can't even land a single one on him.

And what's more, whenever his stones hit me, Tường drops his hands and with sorrow in his voice says something like, "Ok, that's enough now, right? We should stop, brother."

It's a horrible blow to my pride whenever he says that. "No, no stopping!" I snarl back through clenched teeth while heaving more stones.

Tường seems anxious about my rising blood. He keeps going with the game to satisfy me, but his throws start to be more reluctant and the stones veer off in other directions.

Aware that he's intentionally tossing his stones astray rattles me even more. But I don't know how to shed my anger.

Eventually I come up with a plan.

"Ok, fine, I surrender," I say, dejected, dropping my hands to my side.

Tường is delighted. He's been waiting for a while to end this unexpected war.

He rushes over to me without an ounce of suspicion, asking with care, "Did you get a bruise anywhere? Let me rub some balm on it for you."

Tường has no idea I'm still gripping a stone in my hand.

Waiting for him to get close, with pursed lips, my arm shoots out.

Completely without warning, so Tường has no time to duck. The stone hits him directly in the temple.

I cross my heart that I didn't mean to throw it at Tường's head. I just acted out of aggravated rage.

Tường falls to the ground and covers his head.

"Oooo ouch!"

I sprint over to him in a panic and take his hands from his head. My voice filled with worry, I say, "Move your hands and let me see what's happening."

Tường uncovers his head, my face turns grey to see his bloody fingers.

"Oh, dammit! You're bleeding!"

Tường is worried. "Is it a lot?"

"A bit," I lie. And while one hand of mine applies pressure to his head wound, the other supports his back.

"Ok, just try to stand up. I'll walk you back inside and find some treatment for you."

Tường steps beside me, whimpering, "Why'd you throw a stone at me? You said 'surrender'!"

"That's just the pseudo-surrender, it means I pretend I'm

surrendering, you understand?" I try to justify myself. "In fights, one should take advantage of every trick in order to win. It's what all the talented generals do."

Tường, in awe, listens to me bragging. He even forgets about the stinging pain at his temple and gasps with admiration. "Wow, your trick is so good! I didn't suspect anything. I am sure you will make a great general if you join the army one day."

"For sure!"

My gut is filled with regret. I deceived and hurt my little brother, but he still trusts me so innocently, even my most exaggerated bragging.

I walk him along the fence, my head swirling with ideas of how to make it up to him. I promise myself: if Tường ever gets into trouble, like if a beating from my dad is coming because he didn't do his schoolwork, I will volunteer to get punished. I will tell my dad that I am the one who tempted him to play outside . . .

A booming voice suddenly ruptures the nice thoughts running through my head.

"So you two weaseled away from naptime and got up to something?"

No need to look up. The cold metal voice rubbing at my ear already has me shaking like a leaf, knowing the hell that will soon pour down on my head.

Being caught red-handed by my father while roaming around in the hot afternoon sun is like Death grabbing you by the neck.

That's why, without a word, I immediately let go of Tường and take off sprinting toward my grandma's house.

I hide out at my grandma's house until it's very dark. When I guess my dad has already gone to sleep, I grope my way through the dark back home.

I creep into my house through the back door, tiptoe into my bedroom, quietly brush the dust from my feet, and sneak inside the mosquito net.

"Is that you, Brother?" Tường whispers.

"Yeah, it's me," I whisper back. "Mom and Dad are asleep, right?"

"Yeah."

"Is your head still hurting?"

"A bit."

Tường releases a sudden "ouch!" while we're talking.

I am startled. "Hey, shhhh! What's up? I didn't touch your head at all."

"But you touched my body."

I suddenly remember. "This afternoon he beat you up good, huh?

"You know already, why ask?"

I shrink into myself, remembering the dog-taming cane that stands in the corner of our house, the many rattan switches stored on the wall. I feel a huge pitying love and tenderness for my little brother. I feel tears biting at my eyes.

"Please don't be mad at me. This afternoon I shouldn't have run away. If dad had beaten the two of us at once, we could've shared the pain. You would've gotten off easier."

"No, you're right to run away, Brother." Tường grabs my hands and holds tight. "You are my big brother. If you stayed, I would've gotten off easier but dad would've killed you."

Tường says not one word of blame and I feel a fierce pang of regret.

I rack my brain for the worst words I can come up with to curse myself. After a few days, when the whole family is out, I convince Tường to go out to the back yard and play cattle poke. But when my father unexpectedly comes home and sees us, I instantly forget all my promises to myself and

I take off out of the gate like I've got three legs and four wings. I leave Tường alone again to bear the punishment.

8.
the story lover

Sometimes I have the impression that I'm the younger one and Tường is the big brother.

Mom often scolds me when I compete with Tường, "You're the older one, you should indulge him."

But in fact, it is totally Tường who indulges me, in both big and little matters.

Tường doesn't fear me at all, even though I bully him. Tường indulges me just because he is the younger one who really loves and adores his brother.

For being a good student, every year I bring home some award.

Tường gently fingers the pencil case, the bundle of notebooks, the colorful shiny paper that I place on the dining table in the middle of the house. He then stares up at me, eyes twinkling with joy, and almost breathless in admiration.

"So cool! I wish one day I could be a good student just like you!"

The kid who does well in school is always the kid who gets the most benefits at home.

My mom often scolds me, often tells me to make sacrifices for Tường. But at home when she needs us to do something, she hardly ever asks me. Running over to Grandma's house to borrow a basket, going over to the neighbor's house to take some straw to line the chicken coop, or going to draw water for the jars—my mom usually sends Tường out to do it. Her only reason: "So your brother can study!"

It is Tường, not me, who completely shoulders the heavy and light work at home and yet still mostly keeps a joyful look on his face, not complaining even one sentence.

Because he shares my mom's reasoning: "So Brother can study!"

Most of the time, except when dad's in a rage and unleashes the switch on my body, I am none other than a little king of the house, not having to lift a finger to do anything. And when dad goes job hunting in the city, only coming back home on the weekends, the onslaught of switches is almost completely stopped.

With all of this going on, I keep on becoming a better student and Tường keeps on becoming a worse student.

With all the burdens to shoulder, Tường has little time to touch his homework. But he sees this as his unlucky fate, which he accepts with ease just as long as I keep studying to reach higher education and eventually become a doctor or engineer, or if there is ever a hostile wartime, to become a general and make him proud.

Yes, Tường is sluggish with his studies, but he gets completely engrossed in reading.

While I never touch a book unless it's for school, Tường doesn't go anywhere without folding a book into his pocket. And, if his trousers don't have pockets, he'll stick the book into his belt.

Whenever he's got a moment of free time, he'll pull out a book and glue his face to every word. To him, stretching out in the grass hour after hour to read is something unmeasurably marvelous. He even reads sitting at the edge of the well, or sitting with his legs dangling from the guava tree in the back of the garden.

Every time I happen to encounter this scene, I wag my finger at him. "Aren't you scared of breaking your neck, Tường?"

Snow White and the Seven Dwarfs, Sleeping Beauty, Cinderella, and a bunch of other stories. Tường has memorized every last detail of them.

Of course, I also know those stories. But I've only heard them from either Dad or Uncle Dan. To read by myself, stumbling page by page through books thick with words just to gather up the crumbs of a story and pack them into my memory, is a pain.

Tường's passion for reading naturally brings some benefit to me.

I don't need to touch a single book and I can still know so many good stories.

At night, when the two of us are in bed under the covers, I usually can convince him to tell me a story. I listen and fall asleep whenever I lose interest.

The next night I'll ask, "Where did you leave off last night, Tường?"

9.
the story of the Fire-Bellied Toad

Tường reads so many interesting books. He especially likes *The Fire-Bellied Toad*, though I feel this story is so stupid.

The story is about a young man who comes from a very poor family but is a diligent student.

By day, the student goes into the forest and gathers firewood to sell so he can have money to buy rice and lamp oil. By night, he gets completely wrapped up in reading until the neighborhood chickens let out their second cry around 2 a.m., then he sleeps.

(Surely he is reading textbooks to prepare for his exams, not reading stories like the guy Tường).

He lives in just a small hut. His total belongings are one curved knife and a stack of books.

The only one who makes friends with him is a fire-bellied toad. When he's studying late into the night, the toad will hop around under his feet, snapping up all the mosquitoes that are buzzing about.

(Tường especially likes this part. He can recite by heart the paragraph in a lovely sing-song voice.)

Then comes the day he journeys to the capital to sit for his examination, and the fire-bellied toad follows along. On the road, he uses the spirit jewel of the fire-bellied toad to rescue a friend who turns out to be a bad guy.

When this friend learns of the toad's jewel's life-restoring powers, he plots to steal the jewel.

At this time, a princess in the palace falls critically ill. The King and Queen rush to call a royal physician to come and save her, but all the royal physicians are helpless before the task. The King hastily hangs a scroll announcing his search for a reputable doctor, and the news spreads throughout the city: "Whoever can save the life of the Princess will be chosen as a prince."

The news reaches the fire-bellied toad. The toad says to the student, "This is our chance to find the thief and take back the jewel."

The next day, the thief, masquerading as a reputable doctor, enters the palace to treat the Princess while the student and the fire-bellied toad follow behind and look for a way to mix in with the officials.

When inside the palace, the bad-guy friend takes the jewel from his pocket and places it on the nose of the Princess, but the Princess continues to lie there motionless before the anxious King and Queen.

Meanwhile, the student emerges from the crowd and advances toward the King, speaking and pointing into the face of the thief.

"Your Majesty, before all else please imprison this man here."

He takes the jewel, then points to the fire-bellied toad, now sitting squarely in his palm, illuminating for all to see that the life-restoring jewel's powers can only be exercised by the spirit toad. He indicates that the person is a thief who does not know the jewel is only effective if the spirit toad agrees.

Shortly after, the student gently places the jewel on the nose of the Princess. As expected, the princess suddenly stirs and gradually recovers consciousness before the rejoicing crowd.

The ending, of course, is always the same::

"After the Princess's life is saved, the King receives the student as the Prince."

After that, his exam performance is the most outstanding in the field and he is awarded first place.

Later he goes on to become a chancellor in the royal court.

10.
Little Boy

I can't understand how Tường can like such a stupid story so much.

It's the same every time: whenever I ask him to tell me a story, the first one will be of *The Fire-Bellied Toad*.

"No! Tell a different one!" I throw my hands up. "*The Fire-Bellied Toad, The Fire-Bellied Toad*, all the time!"

Tường will then tell a different story. But not even two days later, after the two of us wipe the dust from our feet and enter the mosquito net to sleep, he again draws out the *Fire-Bellied Toad* story.

He is so obsessed with that toad that I force myself to

give the direct statement, "From now on, I demand that you never again tell me the story of *The Fire-Bellied Toad*, not even once more, Tường!"

Then comes the day I happen to see a toad under our bed and I can start to understand why Tường loves the story so much.

The toad I meet is, of course, not a fire-bellied one. Uncle Dan told us that fire-bellied toads only live up in the mountains or in the grassy banks of ponds or lakes, and they have purple, red, or yellowish-red skin.

The toad sits before me and is typical of all the toads I've seen: grayish dry skin full of warts, sitting like an athlete in the ready position on a starting line for a hundred-meter dash. When I squat in front of the toad with my curious gaze, it also lifts its protruding eyes and thoughtfully observes me, as if wondering who I am and why it only sees me just now.

Tường enters while I am carefully watching the toad.

"You're raising a toad, eh?" I ask.

"Yeah."

"Where'd you get it from?"

"He's been living here for a while, you just didn't see. His cave is right under the foot of our bed," Tường answers, and drops about seven or eight fly corpses he's just hunted, a fly swatter made of bamboo still in his hand.

"Your meal, Little Boy!"

The toad jumps up, its sharp and short tongue flicks in and out as fast as lighting, and in the blink of an eye, the bunch of flies vanish.

"Is Little Boy its name?"

"Yes, I gave him that name. He is a little boy but also the uncle to the sky gods in the myth," Tường explains and squats next to me, his eyes stuck to Little Boy, who is now turning its back and sluggishly jumping back into its cave after being satisfied by its party of flies.

I am sure it was hungry and that's why it jumped out of the cave to wait for Tường.

I have a thought, and ask, "But it's not at all a fire-bellied toad, is it?"

"Uhm."

"So how can it have the magical life-restoring pearl to give you?"

"Uhm."

I slap his shoulder with a chuckle. "Just don't dream about marrying a princess!"

Tường doesn't respond to my teasing but he asks, with a twinkle in his eyes, "Are princesses real in this life, Brother?"

I rake my hand through my hair, wavering.

"I don't know either. Perhaps they were once upon a time, but not anymore."

11.
sister Vinh

Tường really pampers Little Boy.

Since noticing there's a toad living under our bed, I also notice that Tường goes hunting every day to find food for Little Boy.

Little Boy, of course, still searches for its own food, eating flies, mosquitoes, and common insects. But Tường worries that Little Boy is not getting enough food. He whittles pieces of bamboo and weaves together a swatter to go hunting flies in his spare time.

Tường always gleans the pieces of fallen rice after meals and saves them for Little Boy.

Whenever we hear Little Boy grinding its teeth under the bed at night, without fail there is rain the next morning.

And raining days are always wonderful for us.

While Tường and I go to bathe and play in the rain, Little Boy also excitedly hops out from its space beneath the bed, creeps up to the door, lies in wait, then shoots out its tongue to catch the insects flying across.

When we've had enough of the rain, Tường and I huddle together beneath the gutter to listen to the water pelting down above our heads and imagine we are showering under a majestic waterfall, though I've never seen a waterfall outside of the pictures in textbooks.

After dunking himself in the rain, Tường always comes back in to play with Little Boy and be as helpful as he can, that is, catch those little winged creatures.

Usually at these times, I'll abandon Tường with his toad and hightail it across the way to Sister Vinh's house.

Sister Vinh's house has the biggest tiled roof in the village, and an expansive brick-paved courtyard with an old flame tree casting its shadow over a fence where us kids often gather to play hopscotch, blind man's bluff, games of play capture, and all our other favorite games.

Sister Vinh is six years older than me.

While I'm only a thirteen-year-old boy, she's a beautiful young lady, though a bit thin. She has rosy fair skin, thick black hair that drapes all the way down her back, and when she smiles, her eyes crinkle up and look like two minus signs with long, long tails.

I like it most when she smiles.

And even better, she often smiles at me, though in her yard there is always a bunch of kids racing around, jumping and screaming beside me.

The reason Sister Vinh often smiles at me is that she likes Uncle Dan.

Tường himself told me so.

"You remember how Uncle Dan's always standing under the flame tree in front of Sister Vinh's house and humming into his harmonica all night?

"I remember."

I can recall my dad at least three times furiously pushing open the door and taking up his cane, barking at my uncle, "You mad, Dan? You trying to keep everyone awake here?"

Uncle Dan would then jet out of there at superhuman speed.

Tường declares, as if a connoisseur on the subject, "This is how Uncle Dan reveals his love to Sister Vinh."

I shrug. "You are just a little baby, how would you know?"

"Uncle Dan is the one who told me!"

"Revealing his love by the harmonica?"

"Yeah."

Well, if Uncle Dan told him so, it must be true! I am silent for a while, and then ask again, and then get confused again.

"So why haven't I seen Uncle Dan humming into his harmonica beneath the flamboyant tree for this whole month, do you know?"

It turns out that the guy Tường had the same question before.

He smacks his lips. "I asked him already."

"What'd he say?"

Tường giggles. "He said Sister Vinh is already crazy about him and he doesn't need to 'gnaw the corn' and dry out his throat every night anymore."

12.

the bluebird

Sister Vinh is crazy about Uncle Dan not just for his harmonica playing.

She is also crazy about him for his steamy love letters.

Again, this is what Tường tells me. The guy Tường has a
knack for never telling stories all in one stretch. Every story is
like this—one day he'll open it a bit, the next day he'll open
it a bit more. With so many of his stories, by the time I listen
to the ending, I have already clean forgotten the beginning.

The person who carries the letters for Uncle Dan is, of
course, Tường.

I don't understand why Uncle Dan doesn't ask me. I'm
jealous when thinking about it, but then I can explain it to
myself like this: Sister Vinh's father is Teacher Longan, the
head of my class. Uncle Dan doesn't appoint me to carry the
letters perhaps because he worries I'd be scared out of my
wits by my teacher and something would go wrong.

When I listen to Tường, I can see how Uncle Dan is quite
thorough.

Uncle Dan writes a letter, stuffs it into an envelope, then
flips up Tường's shirt and stuffs the envelope into his waistband, hiding it completely in his clothes.

In the afternoon, Tường runs to Sister Vinh's house, calling out loudly, "Sister Vinh! Hey, Sister Vinh!"

Sister Vinh steps out. "What's going on, dear?"

Uncle Dan has laid out for Tường everything he should
say in reply.

"Can you please give my mom one chili pepper?"

"Can you please give my mom one lime?"

"Can you please let my mom borrow one bottle of soy
sauce?"

"..."

According to all of Tường's requests, Sister Vinh hands him one chili pepper, one lime, one bottle of soy sauce, while with the other hand she flips up his shirt and takes out the envelope then thrusts it inside her shirt.

"So you pass by her house but Teacher Longan doesn't know anything?" I wonder.

"Oh, he knows alright."

I bite my lip. "So the teacher doesn't ask anything about it?"

"No, he does. Sometimes the teacher asks, 'Where are you going there, Tường?' Once he asked, 'Why are you coming around like this looking for Sister Vinh?'"

My neck coils back.

"If I were you, for sure I'd have peed my pants then."

"The teacher just sits in his house asking through the wind is all."

"Sitting in the house or sitting anywhere, it's still the same." My neck coils back again and I gently quiver. "Any time I hear my teacher's voice rise, I could just faint."

Tường chortles. "Heh, you scaredy-cat!"

Being criticized, I explode, "No, you are so stupid! Because your teacher is Ms. Peony. If you studied under Teacher Longan like me, just consider if you'd be a scaredy-cat or not!"

13.
in which the bluebird meets danger

Uncle Dan calls the passing of letters between a man and a lady "making bluebirds."

He praises Tường—"You're the best bluebird in the world"—which tickles Tường with joy.

But this best bluebird in the world also has days of meeting danger.

The story of Tường meeting danger is one that he only shyly tells a full week later. As I said already, there's not a single story this guy can bear to tell all at once.

The time was like every other time: Tường crammed Uncle Dan's letter into his waistband then buzzed off to Teacher Longan's house.

"Sister Vinh! Hey, Sister Vinh!"

Tường was standing outside in the yard, screaming loudly. But this time, he didn't see Sister Vinh anywhere.

The person who came out from within the house was Teacher Longan.

Only when seeing the teacher's hard stare did Tường instantly learn what it meant to be scared. Completely startled, his guts slipped and spun away as if floating off to nowhere. He suddenly remembered the two-headed dragon standing watch over the golden apple orchard in the story he'd just read and could only bring himself to peek up at the neck of the teacher's shirt, trembling with anxiety, waiting for a second head to sprout.

"Why are you coming looking for Sister Vinh like this?"

Teacher Longan moved closer and raised his voice, his words like metal.

Tường, with a guilty look, glanced down at the front of his shirt then back up at the teacher.

"Yes, I was asking if you could please give my mom one lime, please?"

The light of Tường's eyes exposed him, he tells me later. Following Tường's line of sight, Teacher Longan's hand reached into and felt around under Tường's shirt.

The teacher took out the letter from the back of Tường's pants then turned on his heels back into his house, not saying a word.

Face paled green as a banana leaf, Tường stood frozen in the middle of the sunny yard for several minutes, arms and legs stiff as wood, wanting only to drop dead.

When it was possible for him to finally stir, he burst into tears.

Tường ran home, still not able to stop sobbing when Uncle Dan, who was waiting in the banana bushes out back, reached out to hug him.

"Shh shh, hey, little guy, what on earth happened?"

At Uncle Dan's question, Tường let out a louder scream. The question was like the blade of a knife boring into his heart's wound, if it were possible to say that his mishap had warranted the name of a "heart wound." And so he cried in uncontrollable sobs, tears gushing out like a broken faucet.

Uncle Dan pulled up Tường's shirt and didn't see the letter anywhere. After some consideration, he gently asked, "So, you didn't meet Sister Vinh, then?"

"Yes . . . no . . ." Tường answered through his tears.

Uncle Dan sighed. "Ok, enough crying."

Tường kept on crying, though. Perhaps he wanted to stop but simply could not. A person cries just like rain falls from the sky: only when out of water does the rain let up, and do we stop crying.

The little guy Tường was just that way, crying and crying without stop. But little by little the sounds of his sobbing grew fainter, the episode moved into whimpering, and then it was complete.

And he was free to sputter, "Teacher Longan . . ."

Uncle Dan touched Tường's head. "I know, I know. You don't have to say anything more."

Then Uncle Dan stood up. "Let me tear out a piece of paper and fold you an airplane."

The idea of Uncle Dan's paper airplane made Tường's face blossom. He was soon shooting the airplane around to

glide in twists and turns through the garden and quickly for-
got the teardrops that had so recently soaked his cheeks.

I click my tongue when Tường finishes his story.

"You're so stupid. It wasn't that Teacher Longan saw your
eyes and then knew you were hiding something in your clothes."

Tường is bewildered. "The teacher knew it from before,
then?"

I kick my leg into his leg, as if knowingly. "I think that
he has known for a long time already. Nobody goes around
asking for one chili pepper, one lime, and one bottle of soy
sauce all the time like that. Only a fool!"

14.
in which
windy rain is the sickness of the sky

One day, I ask Tường out of curiosity, "You remember how
many letters you've passed for Uncle Dan?"

Tường presses his lips together, hesitating. "About ten-
something."

"That many?"

"Yes."

I squint. "Was there ever a time you secretly opened a letter to see what Uncle Dan had written inside?"

"One time," Tường answers with some embarrassment,
his face blushing as if suddenly covered in a layer of sunset.

I move closer to him. "What'd he write?"

"It seems a poem."

"Poetry?"

"Yes."

"What poetry?"

"I don't know."

"So any lines you remember?"

"I remember two lines."

"Tell me then."

Tường says:

Windy rain is the sickness of the sky / Missing her is the sickness of my love.

I don't know if it's the poetry of Nguyễn Bính, but I find the two lines nice, lovely, and I keep saying them under my breath to not forget.

For several days I don't know what to do with the lines, until I suddenly remember Little Beg, who sits beside me in class.

Beg is lovely, her two cheeks are full of freckles. She and I and the guy Sơn, the son of Old Man Huấn, share one desk. I am in the middle, she's on the right, the guy Sơn's on the left.

The guy Sơn and I tease her every day. During lessons, I'll turn to her and ask, "You want to eat something, hey, Beg?"

"Eat what?"

"Beg to eat!"

Later it's the guy Sơn's turn. "Oh, I'm so hungry! You want to eat something, Beg?"

"Eat what?"

"Beg to eat!"

Being teased as "beggar," Beg always cries. She gets upset and turns her face away from us, without saying a word.

But she's a forgetful one. Just one day later, she's easily trapped again by our game. When I ask, "You want to eat something, Beg?" she quickly responds, "Eat what?" And then tears swell in her eyes. For the whole class. Thousands of times like that.

It means thousands of times I see her crying.

And then on the thousandth time plus one, it occurs to me that I can't stop teasing Little Beg because I'm nuts about her sullen anger. Many girls when things are normal look like nothing special, and I'm not sure how but they become so loveable when they get angry and upset.

15.

the greedy one

I decide to send those two "nice and lovely" lines to Little Beg.

I don't know why, but I can't stop myself from doing it.

Perhaps I want to imitate Uncle Dan.

In my fresh-born soul, if I was Uncle Dan, Sister Vinh would definitely be Little Beg.

I take some pages from my notebook, carefully write down the lines on a white page, then fold it into quarters and put in an envelope.

I don't thrust the letter in Little Beg's hand, though it'd be really easy to do so, because I'd love to do everything one hundred percent the same as Uncle Dan.

During recess, I pull the guy Sơn to the back of the yard, take the letter out from my pocket, and hand it to him.

"Later when we're back to class, you can help me give this letter to Little Beg then."

"What letter? You can just do it yourself, can't you?"

"No," I say, with an experienced tone. "For such kinds of letters people should rely on 'the bluebirds.'"

"The bluebirds?" The guy Sơn is baffled. "What's a bluebird?"

I scratch my head. "The bluebirds are special letter carriers."

I slap Sơn on the shoulder, an act I hope can extinguish his series of questions that are surely unanswerable. "You are my bluebird."

Fearing his refusal, I raise my voice and exaggerate. "Being a bluebird is really cool! Not everyone can be a bluebird. Gotta be super excellent to be one."

"Nonsense!"

The guy Son sucks his teeth at me but doesn't deny it. He raises his beady eyes to look at me, his voice smelling of greed. "So what do I get for being a bluebird?"

"What you get . . ." I falter, completely not expecting this kind of question.

"Yeah," the guy Son says straightforwardly. "To carry the letter for you I should surely get paid with something!"

I stuff my hands into my pockets, my gut wishing that the hanged ghost at Son's house would've taken his soul a long time ago!

My hands fish around in my pockets a bit and then reappear with a handful of colorful marbles.

Country kids don't have as many games as city kids. We still play with marbles and all those childish things even when we're grown up enough.

"Look at this!" I show him the handful of marbles. "You can take the one you like!"

Son raises his eyes, inspecting them closely, picking out each marble one by one to see. Licking his lips, he says, "I like all the marbles."

"What?" I roll my eyes.

"I will take all of them." Son fixes his jaw.

"I can beat you, Son!" My cheeks inflame and my face hardens. "I worked all week to win these marbles. What's left for me to play with if you take them all?"

"If you disagree then we're done." Son turns to go. "Pass the letter to Little Beg yourself."

I tensely look at the "bluebird," confusion twisting my stomach in knots.

Such a story will be nothing without a bluebird, and worse, I won't resemble Uncle Dan.

Eventually I scream out, "I agree!"

I regretfully pour all the marbles from my hand over to Sơn's. My voice full of loathing, I say, "Such a greedy one!"

16.
the foolish nonsense

After recess, the guy Sơn is a few grams heavier with one letter in his shirt pocket and a handful of marbles in his pants pocket.

But he moves very quickly.

To tell the truth, it's really because I move slowly.

Three of us at the table: Little Beg sits beside the wall, then comes me, then next comes Sơn. If we just go to our seats in this order, I will block the guy Sơn's path.

That's why I lag behind, keeping my eyes locked on the "bluebird" every second.

I imagine he's awfully embarrassed. Without warning the guy Sơn does his "duty" in the blink of an eye. He takes the letter out from his pocket and flings it before Little Beg's face. With chin stuck out and a curt voice he says, "Here's yours, Little Beg, you got that?"

"What's this letter?" Little Beg tenderly inspects the letter.

"The guy Thiều wants to give it to you."

Finished speaking, Sơn turns on his heels and hustles away, clearing a path for me to come in. Compared to Tường's hard work when carrying the letters for Uncle Dan, the effort that Sơn puts into my story is as tiny as a grain of sand. His snippy and abrupt attitude is so careless. The story of a young boy's first time sending a letter to a girl is majorly meaningful, but his gestures are utterly absurd, sloppy words just punching the listener's ears.

But I don't have time to regret the loss of some marbles.

I stealthily sit in my spot, not daring to look at Little Beg. But from the corner of my eye I'm still anxiously following her every move and nearly holding my breath when seeing her gently tear open the envelope and take out the letter.

Naturally I am completely in the dark about what Little Beg will do after reading the two lines of poetry I wrote for her. Too childish to imagine the steps of romance and whether my letter could open a little love story.

I am only imitating Uncle Dan. And imitating him only halfway.

It's like I copy his homework of love exercises but only the beginning part. The middle and the ending parts are being covered by his hand. And so, I cannot guess the developments to come in the story. I daydream, *Surely Little Beg will write some note back to me?*

I think and think, bite my lips. I guess Little Beg will do this or that. I envision the worst consequences: she crumples the letter into a ball and throws it back in my face.

I sit breathlessly in my chair, imagining all sorts of crazy things, except the one thing I could never have imagined: Little Beg doesn't swear at me, doesn't throw the letter back in my face. Instead she takes the letter and walks directly up to the teacher's desk. Against my luck, it is the gruff Mr. Longan's literature class that we're in at this moment.

The outcome is clear: Mr. Longan calls on me to rise to the board and before all the eyes of my curious classmates, he seizes my ear and excruciatingly pinches it, almost lifting my whole body off the ground.

His teeth grinding, he says, "Loser love! Can't write a simple sentence without making a complete mess, but here copying some lines of foolish love nonsense!"

17.

dear, what to do if our dreams don't come true?

After that accident, I stay angry with Little Beg for months.

I don't so much as look at her in class, let alone talk to her. While doing our recitions, she accidentally bumps my elbow and I immediately push her arm back in a cold, ungentle way.

And I stop going over to her house to play, though her house is one of only two playing places for us kids in the village, with a yard for drying grains that's almost as big as Sister Vinh's brick courtyard. On nights when the moon was bright, if not going by Sister Vinh's house, me and my friends would gather around Little Beg's house to play blind man's bluff, capture the flag, leeches and turtles, and so on, until it was so dark that we couldn't see, and sometimes we'd just wait for our parents to take their switches out in search of us and we'd have to flee along the hedges back toward home.

Little Beg knows I'm angry with her and she's sad about it.

Sometimes, glancing over to my right side, I rejoice to see her face looking like it's about to cry, the freckles on her cheek nearly trembling.

Sometimes when seeing her mopey expression, my heart cannot hold back a wavering feeling, but I am determined not to make up with her.

With a face full of tears, I went back to my seat after suffering Mr. Longan's punishment and Little Beg was worried about me, her voice flooded with regret. "Hey, I'm sorry! I couldn't imagine Mr. Longan was going to punish you like that."

"You can stuff your sorry!" I said furiously. "What were you thinking? Bringing my letter over to the teacher?"

"I didn't think anything. I supposed you were trying to tease me with it so I went and told the teacher is all."

"Are you blind?" I was becoming increasingly irritated. "When have I ever teased you?"

Little Beg was so scared her face turned green. Surely she saw my jaw pulsing like it was getting ready to chew on her bones. With lowered eyes she stammered, "So what did you give me the letter for?"

At that point I was stuck. How to explain to her? I'm sure Sister Vinh would never have asked Uncle Dan a stupid question like that.

"You really are a baby!" I finally exhaled and my sulking let up a bit. "I will not play with you anymore."

Actually I'm not angry with Little Beg for very long. I know she didn't intend to hurt me. But all the teasing from my friends makes it impossible for me to make peace with her.

Everywhere I go, their toxic mouths meet me chanting: *An old lady fakes out an old man down by the banks of the hanky panky.*

Even the guy Sơn relentlessly carves into my wounded heart: *Dear, what to do if our dreams don't come true? Buy some pills and swallow them all to be through.*

For a long time, life is like this.

18.

teacher Longan

I only stop feeling angry at Little Beg on the day when Teacher Longan takes the rattan switch and goes in search of Uncle Dan and Sister Vinh.

He walks around the porch of my house, a hot tongue in his mouth. "Where's Dan? Come out here! I have something to say!"

It is evening, and the guy Tường and I are squatting on the floor.

The two of us were calling Little Boy out for some left-over rice when Teacher Longan's voice suddenly scattered bullets across our ears.

Because after dinner my mom usually heads to my grand-ma's to discuss the ceremony of my grandpa, there are only the two of us left at home.

Our insides are choked with fear as we look at each other.

"Do you know where Uncle Dan is?" I whisper.

Tường's worry is the same as mine. His voice flattens as if streaming out from a broken speaker. "Uncle Dan and Sister Vinh must be sitting down by the bank now."

The bank Tường mentions flows around behind Teacher Longan's house, next to a rice paddy. Tường and I sometimes go there and inspect what points of the bank between the paddies are best to set our fish traps.

I hear my insides melting as I say, "Sitting there together, they're dead meat if Teacher Longan sees them!"

"Don't worry!" Tường calms me with his own trembling voice. "Teacher Longan is making such a racket over here al-ready, Uncle Dan and Sister Vinh must've heard him already and have enough time to get away."

"Where's Dan hiding?" Teacher Longan's voice booms like thunder and echoes in the immensity. "If I catch you, you're dead!"

My body shrinks into itself. My spirit is like a cowardly soldier who is out of bullets for his gun, with his knife lost, surrounded by enemies ready to attack.

The enemy attacks for real. After screaming in vain for a while, Teacher Longan storms in the house wildly. His voice is like a waterfall, shaking the roof that's about to collapse. "Where did you take my little Vinh to hide, Dan?"

Teacher Longan stands in the middle of the house, furi-ously scanning his eyes around the room, from left to right.

I can see clearly his quivering cheeks, and I would not be surprised if his body starts to produce smoke.

Catching only me and Tường huddled together on the ground, imobile, he lowers his voice. "Why are you guys sitting there? Anyone see the guy Dan around?"

I swallow, force myself to act and look like a good boy. "Dear teacher, I don't know, ah."

"Hmmm, don't know!"

While growling and groaning, Teacher Longan sees Tường and suddenly recalls his crime of being an accomplice in Dan's story. He raises the switch in a feverish rage and whips Tường's back.

"For the 'bluebird,' then!"

The action happens so quickly and decisively that Tường can't possibly avoid it. I hear a *smack!* and see the guy Tường's entire body flap on the ground. He doesn't utter a word but his face reveals the pain.

Dumbstruck, it dawns on me that the teacher has slid his eyes over to where I'm sitting. In the light, I can see red veins popping in his eyes. I force myself up and leap over to the door before his switch reaches my body. His biting words ring out, "And this guy too! '*Windy rain is the sickness of the sky!*'"

After this, I understand why Teacher Longan twisted my ear so painfully that day—not because he hates me but because he's mad at Uncle Dan.

Surely he read the two lines by Nguyễn Bính in the letter that Uncle Dan sent to Sister Vinh. Little Beg's telling on me just happened to ignite the angry bomb in my teacher's soul.

19.

in which Teacher Longan beats Uncle Dan

I still remember when I was eight, an old fortune-teller passed by my house to ask for some mineral water.

With torn clothes, a thin and ragged body, a stubbly beard, and a face like he's only eaten pickles his whole life, he sits cross-legged on a chair, gently drinking water sip by sip from a plastic cup while tilting his eyes and watching me and my brother.

For me, it only takes a few sips to finish one cup of water, but he keeps drinking so slowly and patiently for the whole evening. He doesn't part his lips to speak even a single word while drinking.

However, before leaving he points his finger at me, nods, and says to my mom, "Careful with that boy, he could drown one day!"

I hear his sure words without feeling any emotion stir in me, but my mom turns green as a leaf. Her forehead only relaxes when he adds, "After eighteen years old, if he has survived death from rivers and streams, he'll live a long life."

The old man then turns to look at Tường.

"As for this guy, he's got an envious beauty and his fate will be hard. But he'll be nobly assisted and you don't have to worry so much about him. Though many accidents will befall him, he will be able to endure all in the end."

I don't know what percentage of the fortune-teller's pronouncement is correct. But just the part about Tường meeting many accidents, as I recall them all now, I have to admit that he was right.

Tường's body was beaten by my father's cane, then his head was split open by my stone throwing, and then his back took the switch of Teacher Longan's rage. All unexpected misfortunes flying in from somewhere.

I am the one who is worse behaved, does more wrong things, and always plays more games, but thanks to my fast legs, I can usually escape the beatings.

That time of Teacher Longan's visit, I hide outside for a long while, waiting for him to leave before sneaking back in.

The guy Tường is still sitting there on the ground. He and Little Boy are facing each other. The toad is engrossed in catching prey while Tường is engrossed in weeping.

Looking at him snuffling his little cries, I feel I can't hold my heart together. I sit next to him, put my arms around his shoulders, and try to comfort him. "Don't cry, little boy!"

I am always used to calling Tường "that guy," but spontaneously now I call him "little boy" and the sweetness of that makes his heart soften a bit more and he weeps even louder.

I rub his back gently and carefully, as if I'm touching something too fragile and easily broken. "Hurts a lot, little bro?"

"Starting to hurt a little less, Brother." Tường cries through sniffles.

"So what's got you still crying nonstop?"

"Why did Teacher Longan beat me for no reason?" Tường lifts his wet face, looks at me, and then swipes away his tears with both hands, still hurt.

"When he caught me red-handed giving letters to Sister Vinh, why didn't Teacher Longan beat me then? Why do it now?"

I sigh. "It's not that Teacher Longan was beating you, little bro. He was beating Uncle Dan."

20.

in which cicada-catching season approaches

So Teacher Longan's beating of Uncle Dan leaves Uncle Dan unscathed and Tường's back bruised purple.

The next morning I lift up his shirt and see that the dark marks have faded, though a vaguely blue-green eel now slithers across his back.

"Hey, Tường." My voice is soft.

"What, Brother?"

"Cicada season's almost here."

"Yes."

"When the summer comes, that means the chorus of cicadas is coming. I'll show you how to lie very still and catch those hummers."

"Cool! We catch them with the sticky pus of jackfruits, right?"

"Yeah, the sticky pus. I'll sharpen two superlong sticks. One stick for you, one stick for me. Then we dip them into the sticky pus."

"I already know! Just like last year!"

Last year the two of us every day at noon would poke along the fence to catch cicadas under the blazing sun. The summer sun would fall in shafts down on the dry yellow leaves of Old Man Huấn's house, the longan bushes in Mr. Longan's house, the star apple tree in my grandmother's garden, and the bronzed hair of me and my brother.

In those afternoons spent hunting cicadas, our faces would flush red and our hair would get singed raggedy like two straw brooms. My mom's shriek was like a battle cry, threatening to call our dad, making us quiver in fear. But come the next day, we'd again sneak back out during the noontime nap, sticks in hand, and pace along the fence listening for the din of cicadas humming up in the tall trees.

But this summer isn't exactly the same as last summer. Last summer, like all the summers before, the one who sharpened the sticks was always the guy Tường.

"Brother, you go and study, let me do it for you!" Tường would say, knife dangling in his hands. At such times, I'd be perfectly content to let him care for the sticks, even though school was out and my only occupation was playing, nothing at all to study for.

But this summer, I insist on sharpening the sticks for us. I want to reciprocate. As the fortune-teller said, Tường is fated to a life of toil and will meet many mishaps. I want to shoulder for my little brother at least one of his struggles. And among his onerous work, the least onerous is sharpening the sticks to hunt cicadas.

But the flame tree in Sister Vinh's front yard hasn't bloomed yet, summer is taking a long time to arrive. I click my tongue in disappointment and look at Tường.

"Guess I'll go look for the chicken grass now."

"To have chicken fights?"

"Yeah."

"I know a place!" Tường's voice rings out. "Let me show you!"

As soon as he says that, Tường takes my hand and drags me out of the house. We shuffle along the stone well behind the garden.

I tag along behind him, my heart sad (so sad). It's always like this: whenever I feel moved to help Tường with something, in the end he's the one who helps me. Again and again like this.

21.

in which a dragonfly bites a belly button

The land surrounding the stone well is perpetually damp and so there are wild plants growing year-round. Gingergrass and trailing daisies flourish alongside amaranth, purslane, and sometimes magenta cockscomb.

The plants grow thickly all around the well.

A bit further, there is a plot of morning glory with plush green leaves. There's more cockscomb growing in that spot between the grasses and the vegetable patch. I don't know how Tường discovered this place. Whenever I pick cockscomb, I just stay close to the fence.

While I'm agonizing over which blades of cockscomb are the longest and the strongest, at the moment having picked enough to fill one hand, the guy Tường seems like he hasn't picked a single blade.

I see him sitting, his body curled over in deep observation of something in his hand.

"What the hell are you sitting for? Why don't you get up and pick some blades of cockscomb, Tường?"

"Come see, Brother!" Tường turns toward me, his hand opened, still squatting on his heels.

Seeing his brightly shining face, I wet my lips and ask, "You got a fire grasshopper?"

"No."

I come closer to peer down and see a millipede curled up in the palm of Tường's hand.

"Oh, gross!" I grimace. "You play with those bugs?!"

"It's a millipede, Brother. They are gentle and good bugs."

Some spit splutters from my mouth as I say, "A millipede is still a bug. You're stupid to play with them, I'm not playing with you anymore."

At that, I take my handful of cockscomb blades back home, leaving Tường to poke the millipede to his heart's content, admiring the way it wraps up into a frightened ball.

Country kids are friends with all kinds of creatures. Buffaloes, cows, dogs, cats, different kinds of birds and insects. I'm the same. I have some matchboxes and cardboard boxes that I use to keep grasshoppers, crickets, cicadas, and beetles. But not like Tường.

Tường will easily play with ants, dragonflies, fireflies, spiders, millipedes, and caterpillars. Right now he's even raising a toad under the bed.

The way that Tường is friendly with every creature sometimes makes me think that he is not quite normal. With just a stick in his hand, he can passionately frolic for hours with a caterpillar clinging to the piece of wood.

He is like a bug advocate. Whenever I sneer at his friends he'll say, "You just don't know about them. Spiders spin webs so we have something to stop the bleeding when we cut our finger. And the dragonfly bites our belly button to help us learn how to swim."

About spider webs, sure, Tường is right. In the past, whenever my finger got cut open, I'd just stick it in my mouth and run as fast as I could to some storage space or outhouse to find a spider web. With a spider web wrapped around a wound, the bleeding stops, I'm not sure why. For so long among my friends, that's been the magical medicine for a childhood of so many scratches.

But I don't believe for one second the story about dragonflies biting the belly button.

I narrow my eyes at Tường. "You're ridiculous. A dragonfly bites your belly button and you know how to swim?"

"That's right."

"Who told you such a thing?"

"Uncle Dan told me."

"Uncle Dan, eh?" I lower my voice, pausing. "You're telling the truth? Let me go run and ask him, then."

"It's the truth!" Before I can make a move, Tường runs out behind the garden.

A bit later, he's running back with a red dragonfly in hand.

"Lift up your shirt!" Tường urges as he stares enthusiastically at my stomach.

"No." I step back. "Give it your belly button to bite first!"

Tường opens his shirt, places the dragonfly in the middle of his belly.

I put both hands on my knees and strain to see. I see the dragonfly lift its two fragile wings and hooked tail. There isn't time for a close inspection before the guy Tường is screaming out in fear, hands frantically ripping the dragonfly off his body.

"What's the matter?" I panic. "It hurts that much?"

An embarrassed smile creeps over his face. "It hurts medium. Just like an ant bite is all."

"It hurts medium but you make an earth-shattering scream like that?"

I give Tường a doubtful look. It seems like he's about to cry from the pain.

And so then Tường shares the dragonfly with me—"Your turn now"—and my hand snaps back.

"I'm not playing your stupid game!"

"Stupid?"

"Even stupider than stupid!" I shrug. "When I see you swimming I'll believe it."

That afternoon, the two of us go down to the stream.

I stand on the bank, Tường walks the edges of the dried-out stream searching for a spot where the water is high enough to try swimming.

In conclusion, the swimming session can be summed up in a piece of sad dialogue between the two of us.

"Can you swim?"

"I can."

"Are you sinking?"

"I'm sunk."

22.

one-handed canoe

I'm chuckling all the way home from the stream. "See! I told you it's a stupid game."

Tường hypothesizes, "Perhaps the red dragonfly does not have the mystical gift. I'll catch a king dragonfly later."

My skin prickles when hearing Tường's words. The king dragonfly is double or triple the size of the red dragonfly, and terrifying. A king dragonfly bites your belly button, your belly is going to have a big hole.

"Stop your stupid playing," I pressure him.

"But Uncle Dan said so!"

It's true that Uncle Dan said so. But then Uncle Dan also says something else.

Tường and I meet Uncle Dan, and tell him about the day Tường learned how to swim. He caresses the head of the little squirt and says regrettably, "Oh, silly! I was kidding. I let a dragonfly bite my belly button once when I was a kid, but I still couldn't swim!"

So it turns out that when he was our age, Uncle Dan was just as foolish as Tường.

"So can you swim now?" Tường blinks his eyes, naively wondering.

Uncle Dan answers by taking the two of us to the stream.

Before our astonished eyes, he takes off his T-shirt and submerges his body in the stream. Just one blink and he disappears under the water.

He glides to the other side of the stream without coming up once for air, then raises his head among a bunch of water banana trees with their deep red flowers blooming by the bank, and gives us a wide and happy smile. "That good?"

Tường claps and claps. "So wonderful! Teach us how to swim, Uncle, please!"

Uncle Dan makes his way back. I could fall on my knees when seeing him swim like that, fast as an otter despite just having one hand to stroke through the water.

That day, Tường and I take turns riding on Uncle Dan's slippery back, so joyful and scared at the same time. Uncle Dan becomes a canoe carrying the two of us back and forth between the banks of the stream. A whole ten times that afternoon!

He didn't teach us how to swim, but just as it was we were still overjoyed.

He says, "This time you guys just go by canoe. Next time I'll teach you to swim."

Before leaving the stream, Uncle Dan picks some wild pineapple leaves by the bank and makes a kazoo for Tường to hum the whole way home. He is trying to make it up to the little squirt for listening to him and inviting dragonflies to gnaw at his navel.

23.

sad harmonica

When Uncle Dan gave Tường the pineapple leaf kazoo, the story of Teacher Longan's rabid hunt for Uncle Dan and Sister Vinh hadn't yet unfolded.

When learning of Tường's causeless beating that hurt him to the bone, Uncle Dan's face turns heavily sad.

He caresses Tường's head again. "Poor dear!"

His voice is low and somber, almost moaning.

He speaks to Tường without looking at him. His sorrowful eyes seem to be meandering elsewhere, beyond the distant row of bamboo trees. His usual cheerful face becomes austere, its animated features suddenly seeming hard as wood.

I sit next to him, my eyes not daring to glance his way, my lips not daring to stir. And Tường acts the same, following Uncle Dan's way of directing his eyes elsewhere, dreamy, wondering.

The anxious atmosphere weighs on my heart.

A harmonica sound rises out of nowhere.

"It's so beautiful!" Tường says. "Uncle, play more!"

I'm eager. "I haven't heard you playing the harmonica for so long!"

But what Uncle Dan plays seems to flatten my soul. The music feels so sad, so sentimental, not like other days.

It's like the music is crying, blaming someone, grieving. Surely he's thinking of Sister Vinh and their forbidden love. Teacher Longan doesn't want his daughter to marry a man with a missing arm.

I blurt out, "Please stop playing."

Tường adds, "It's so sad, Uncle!"

Uncle Dan puts the harmonica into his breast pocket. "Uhm, ok I'll stop playing. Let me tell you some ghost stories, then."

It's afternoon. Ghost stories told by night are better, but Tường and I still get excited. "Yes, right! Uncle, tell us the story about that guy Sơn who wakes up and sees his white shirt turned pink!"

And then Uncle Dan rolls up the sleeve of his amputated arm, a habit, before he tests his voice with some sounds from his throat. "You guys already know, Old Man Huấn has a two-story house . . ."

24.
the ghost tiger

I ask the guy Sơn one day, "If your house has the ghost of someone who hung themselves, how come you're not scared?"

"What're you talking about, the ghost of someone who hung themselves?" Sơn shrugs off the question. "That's just a rumor people tell."

He spits on the ground, his voice rising to rude. "Only stupid kids believe that story."

I'm indignant, though unsure of what's going on. My eyes are round as saucers. "So people are just bluffing, then?"

"Of course."

"So how come I heard about the previous owner of your house having a daughter who married a guy with a gambling problem and when that guy went to prison she was so heartbroken that she hung herself in the house?"

The guy Sơn looks at me like he's looking at a rotten cabbage. His lips tighten across his teeth. "The lady didn't hang herself. She died of typhoid."

"Don't you get it?!" I am nearly shouting, my voice triumphant. "If someone died, that means there's a ghost. So you just deny it and still dare to call me the stupid one."

Embarrassed, like he's been caught red-handed stealing something, Sơn says, "I'm not denying anything."

He clears his throat and his voice recovers its stubbornness. "You're really so stupid."

To my amazement, he carefully explains where my stupidity lies. "Death by typhoid is different from death by hanging. Death by hanging is how you turn into a ghost."

"Actually, you are the stupid one!" I snap into a rage. "Any cause of death turns you into a ghost."

Sơn seems to realize that his argument is unsound. He scratches his neck. "But ghosts from typhoid are the mild ones. Only the ones from hanging haunt you."

On this point, Sơn is correct. I remember Uncle Dan once told me that people who die by hanging have the pervasive smell of air after death, and their souls aren't able to move on so they wreak havoc on the living.

"So the ghost story of someone who hung themselves in your house is made up then, huh?" In the end, my voice calming down, I wonder.

"Yeah, super made up." Sơn swings his arm violently. "Including the story about me chucking my shirt to the ground and running away, and that horseshit about my shirt being sticky with blood."

Though without understanding why, I don't question Sơn's story, even though he just swore at me and called me stupid two times. Perhaps it isn't what he says, but more the look on his face that convinces me.

I wet my lips. "So the story about Lady Thoan going to collect firewood and being kidnapped by a ghost is also made up?"

"Also made up." Sơn shakes his head, his tone of voice is as if I am the only stupid kid in the whole village who doesn't already know the truth like everyone else. "Even the story about the guy Chair going to work in the fields and meeting a ghost too."

Sơn's confirmation gives me immediate relief. Thinking about the immense cemetery behind our house, I gently sigh. "So then, all ghost stories are just made up."

"Ah, you are even more stupid!" Sơn snorts. "I only said those three stories are made up. Behind your house the ghosts are real."

"Behind my house?" My voice trembles as a chill runs down my back. "You mean the ghosts in the cemetery—"

"The cemetery beside your house doesn't have ghosts," Sơn interrupts. "But go all the way to the end of the cemetery and you'll see Withering Grass Hill, right?"

"Yeah."

"So then go to the end of Withering Grass Hill. You know what's there?"

"I don't. I've never gone over there."

Right after I answer, my ears are bracing for more of Sơn's swearing and calling me stupid. But this time he only grins and breaks into a laugh.

"Over there by Withering Grass Hill is Black Cat Hamlet. I also haven't been but I heard my dad talk about it. Black Cat Hamlet used to be a haunted area with bad waters, now a few trees and vegetation have grown in but there're still traces of the old forest. Specifically, a ghost tiger is still there."

"A ghost tiger?" My eyes double in size.

"Yep." Sơn nods, his eyes shifting all over the place, his voice dropping to a hush so I almost have to put my ear in his mouth to hear him more clearly. "In the meager forest of Black Cat Hamlet is one old tiger who got cursed because it ate around a hundred people. My dad told me that once while being hunted it suffered a terrible injury to its leg. After that it became evil and always dreams of revenge."

"So is the cursed tiger any different from a tiger that is not cursed?" I again wet my parched lips and ask in a whisper.

"A cursed tiger can hear people. Some of them can hear from any distance. I bet he knows everything that humans know."

As soon as Sơn speaks he whips his head around as if a three-legged tiger were lying in wait right beside us, which makes me spin around to look in the same direction, my heart fluttering.

I calm myself down by remarking, "But it's not a ghost. Only ghosts are worth fearing. A cursed tiger, however . . ."

"A cursed tiger and a ghost tiger are the same thing. *Cursed* here means *evil spirit*, that kind of ghost demon." Sơn ventures this answer while tilting his head close to my head and whispering through the space in between his teeth. "My dad told me the tiger ghost is super intelligent. If it wants to catch some person, it does it by making the person feel a stomach ache, and when the victim cannot bear to stay inside the house, they have to go outside to poop. The tiger ghost is waiting right by the door and when the victim steps out of the house, it pounces! Never misses its target."

The impact of Sơn's ghastly story sweeps across my face and turns me the color of flour. My body is on the verge of a fever.

While about to curl over in sickness, I suddenly remember one detail, and my eyes brighten. "Ha, you are making something up. If it's true like you said, then how does Mr. Tám Tàng the pig slaughter man dare to build his house in Black Cat Hamlet?"

"You know nothing but keep talking." Sơn spits some saliva through the space in his teeth. "Before moving to butcher pigs, Mr. Tám Tàng practiced the profession of a shaman. Mr. Tám Tàng has an amulet and the ghost tiger cannot touch him."

I can't find any holes in Sơn's story. I wriggle around, his reply still humming in my ear. Perplexed, I brush him away with my hand. "I don't believe you at all. Let me go home and ask my uncle."

25.
the legend of Black Cat Hamlet

Uncle Dan silently listens to my report of everything Sơn said. Upon coming to the end, he still doesn't part his lips to make a sound.

"He's lying, right Uncle?" I'm looking at him in confusion, hesitant to utter anything else.

Uncle Dan is still looking off somewhere up in the sky. There's a moment I feel an inkling of doubt that perhaps he didn't hear my question.

After an oh-so-long time, he clicks his tongue to answer. "Your friend is right, little guy."

"How can he be right?" I ask back in shock, still not believing what has come into my ears, though I think I have heard clearly.

Uncle Dan places his hand on my ear and exhales. "It's right that Black Cat Hamlet has a cursed tiger ghost. You guys should never go over that way."

Tường is sitting beside me and bursts out, "How come you didn't tell us before so we knew about it?"

"Because I didn't think that you guys would have anything to do over in Black Cat Hamlet."

"That tiger ghost knows human language then, Uncle?" Tường asks.

"Yeah, he's quite a smart trickster. Many people know this story."

Uncle Dan's eyes shift back and forth between me and Tường, his face suddenly becoming very serious, "Look here, you guys need to remember. No kids from our village should ever go down to Black Cat Hamlet."

I grab Uncle Dan's hand. "So their moms and dads won't let them go then, Uncle?"

"That's right. Go wherever you want to go, but Black Cat Hamlet is off limits."

Uncle Dan is not kidding us. The next day in class, I pretend to ask Little Plum. "Hey, Plum! Tomorrow do you want to go down to Black Cat Hamlet with me?"

"Oh no! Go down there so the tiger can eat you, eh? I won't dare," she says while drawing back.

I invite Little Beg, and she also shakes her head. "I won't go, too scared."

I pretend to not understand her. "What are you scared of?"

"The tiger ghost."

"Who told you that Black Cat Hamlet has a tiger ghost?"

"My dad." She scrunches up her face. "I so much as set foot there, my dad will beat me good."

Little Beg bringing up her dad is all the proof I need, it's impossible to not believe.

I shake my head. "Yeah, if your dad says so then tomorrow I'll also stay home."

26.
Little Beg's father

Little Beg's father is Mr. Xung, a master of traditional medicine. His house has a long shining black cabinet made out of jackfruit wood with so many compact drawers that it takes up one whole wall. Whenever I go over to Little Beg's house, after having enough fun outside, I'll come inside to see her dad picking herbs and roots to make medicine.

When a person comes to him with an ailment, first thing he does is, with a solemn air, put three fingers across their veins to take the pulse, ask several questions, then open their eyelids for a check before having them stick out their tongue.

He looks majestic at work, like a king whose people obey every tiny thing he asks.

But I don't enter the house to see him give examinations. I wait with excitement for the next part: the medicine selection.

He opens this drawer, takes a handful of kumquat peels, opens that drawer, takes a bunch of licorice. There are so many drawers like these, each with a different kind of herbal medicine.

After choosing all the necessary kinds, in the end he always gets a chair to stand on then reaches above his head into the top drawer and picks out some Chinese dry apples to add to the package of medicine.

The Chinese apple is as small as a thumb, shrivelled dry and dark black, but it's crunchy and super sweet when you bite it. Us kids always go crazy for it.

Inevitably, when seeing my head pop in and out from behind the counter, my wistful eyes watching him, Mr. Xung takes an extra apple and hands it to me kindly. "For you, little guy."

Without fail, if I happen to be there when Little Beg's father is making up someone's medicine, I will get a part of it.

But sometimes Mr. Xung doesn't have a guest. That's when, with a powerful craving for the apple, I will swivel my head back and forth to check if anyone's around, and if not, I'll chance it and climb up to the drawers. The apple drawer is so high that I have to stack three chairs to reach it.

Three times I've succeeded in secretly taking an apple.

The fourth time, while straining on the tips of my toes, the stack of chairs comes tumbling down and I fall with them, my body smacking against the floor and leaving me numb.

Afraid that Mr. Xung might have heard the noise, I hold my breath to suffer the pain silently and limp out to the front yard. Gritting my teeth, I run like the wind back home.

The next day in class, I can't look Little Beg in the face. I brace myself to be called a "secret-eater," or, if she really hates me, she could anoint my head with the word "thief" and I know I'd cry.

But all the while I'm surveilling her, she doesn't do anything strange. Little Beg keeps talking and laughing, as if nothing happened, as if no thief came into her house.

Perhaps Mr. Xung doesn't know it was me who entered his house to steal an apple. Perhaps when seeing the fallen chairs, he thought it was some cats or dogs that knocked them over. I release a sigh and feel lighter. After several days I show up at her house again, totally carefree.

When I've had enough of playing tag and capture the flag with friends outside, I scurry into the house during hide-and-seek so no one notices me.

Mr. Xung's medicine room is deserted, only three little chairs are arranged in a neat row in the corner.

My eyes gaze up at the motionless drawers, wondering if I should stack the chairs again and try one more time.

As I hesitate, my eyes fall upon one of the lower drawers and fix there.

It's the only drawer with a label, one word: APPLE.

Instantly, the air around me freezes, the echoes from the yard fade into silence.

All I can hear is the pounding of my heart in my chest— no, not in my chest. My heart is throbbing somewhere else, lower. Perhaps my heart has just dropped somewhere near my stomach.

My legs and hands go numb for some time. When I can move again, all I can do is tear out of there. Away from Little Beg's house. To the road. Far away. As far as possible.

I'm ashamed, as if caught in the act while looting from the drawer. Even though I know Little Beg's father wasn't blaming anything on me, he intentionally moved the drawer of apples down and labeled it APPLE.

He paves the way for me to steal just because he's worried I'll fall down again if I have to stack the chairs to reach the apples.

I'm not sure why, but I've never thought about stealing his apples since that day!

27.
Little Plum's father

Compared to Little Beg's house, Little Plum's house is closer to mine, just the distance of the cemetery running along main road toward the sea.

But, I've never thought of going over to her house (it's she who often comes over to mine, to borrow my notebooks or get help with difficult homework).

I used to go over to Little Plum's house for my haircuts, but now I just go when my mom asks me (if Tường is not home) to go buy some sugar, fish sauce, duck eggs, soy sauce, or other basic things.

Since Little Plum's father's hair salon closed and transformed into a shop selling odds and ends, no one has seen her father anymore. People suspect that he has leprosy and her mom doesn't dare let him wander around outside. If anyone asks, she'll say he's in the city getting treatment.

It's just me who knows that Little Plum's father is still at home.

One time I went over there to take back a notebook she borrowed from me. She's an oh-so-bad student. She's a year older than me, with a beautiful face but an empty head. These days she's almost always ranked at the bottom of our class.

Whenever a homework deadline approaches, she'll borrow my notebook to copy answers. I asked her once, "Why are you so bad at studying?" She didn't answer, just looked down at her toes. I asked her again, "You never do homework at home, right?" She still didn't answer, but I saw her wiping tears away.

Little Plum's teardrops softened my heart. I watched her face with curiosity, as it seemed as if her soul was flying elsewhere, very far from here. In that moment I wish I hadn't uttered those rude words.

Pausing a bit, I clicked my tongue and shook my head like a fly was on my nose. "Hey, don't be sad. If you haven't finished copying my answers yet, you can keep the notebook. I don't need it back anymore."

"I already copied." Little Plum offered a faint smile.

I scratched the back of my neck, looking at Little Plum like a big question mark. "So why are you crying?"

"I have to care for my dad."

At first I didn't get it, even thinking she might be a little crazy.

"You have to care for your dad?" I mechanically repeated back to her.

"Uhm. That's why I don't have time to review the lessons."

My eyes widened. "Isn't your dad in the city for treatment?"

Little Plum snuffled, her face suddenly seeming to wilt. "My dad's still at home. My mom locks him up in the attic."

Little Plum lowered her voice as if afraid of someone eavesdropping. I had to strain my ears and stare at her lips to guess her words.

"Ah, I see."

My eyes instinctively searched for the attic of her house but were unable to see it as it was in the back. I felt myself tremble after her sudden reveal.

My eyes fell back onto Little Plum's somber face and

lingered there for a while, my heart bewildered. Only when she stopped crying and blew her nose did I start to direct my face elsewhere.

28.
in which I cannot keep secrets

Since learning the secret, whenever I go over to Little Plum's house or drop in to buy something, I have the habit of looking up now, though the attic where her dad stays is hidden by the roof in front.

That day when saying goodbye, Little Plum looked at me with wet eyes. "Remember to keep it a secret, ok?"

"Of course."

My head nodded yes and I realized my voice was more assertive than usual, perhaps partly from her sad story, partly from her eyes suddenly turning grey and cold in the afternoon and making my heart sink.

I was agitated the whole way home, not knowing if Little Plum's mom was right or not, but thinking she must have been crushed to have to do it.

Since then, there have been many times when I've wanted to ask Little Plum how her mom confines her dad, but each time I start to open my mouth, it's like something blocks my throat. I feel that question is so coldhearted, even though it's just because of my burning curiosity.

I suppose I just have to imagine in my head. I envision Little Plum's mom chaining her dad to the foot of the bed or to a column of the house so he's not free to move. Or perhaps she doesn't need to do all that, she can just lock the door so the dad can't get out.

For a long time, my mind is stuck on those images, even

in dreams, to the point that my obsessive worry is perhaps no less than that of Little Plum's.

Not being able to unload such an abnormal story on someone else causes me a horrible grief. But I gave my word to Little Plum already, so I bitterly have to accept that I'm imprisoned in this promise.

But there comes a day when I feel that if I don't talk with someone about this story, I will just die, my body will explode into pieces. I gesture to Tường for him to come to the back of the veranda.

"Is it that important?" Tường looks into my eyes as we sit together on the small stove beside the chicken coop.

"Oh, it's super important."

I give him a quick glance then emphasize every word. "The most important of all important stories I have ever told you."

I see the guy Tường tremble, but I can't tell if it's a real tremble or if he's deliberately doing it.

I close my eyes, as if not wanting to look directly at the secret I'm about to reveal, and hurriedly tell him the story about Little Plum's house.

If I have ever spoken quickly before, it can hardly compare to this—my voice stumbling, at times my tongue too big—but I know if I take my time, perhaps I will not be able to summon enough courage to tell all the gloomy thoughts in my head. And for another reason: I believe that if I speak like the wind, then it's also a way to get the dreadful story over and done with.

The guy Tường lowers his eyes and his face darkens upon hearing me finish the story, as if he's an oil lamp that someone has suddenly turned off.

With his shoulders drooped, it is a long, long time before he opens his mouth. "Sister Plum told you this story, then?"

"Yeah, she told me. While crying. She said she has to

spend the whole day caring for her dad and so she doesn't have time to review her lessons."

"Poor, poor Plum."

I chirp back, "Poor, poor her dad too."

I press my hand to my head, worrying. "I've racked my brain and can't come up with how Little Plum's mom confines her dad."

"I think she must lock the door."

"So she leaves him free inside the room? What happens when he busts down the door, then?"

"Her dad wouldn't do that." Tường brightens at his reply, a bit of pink flushing back to his ashen face.

I look at Tường doubtfully. "You've got no evidence at all—"

"If he wanted to, Sister Plum's dad would've already screamed out for someone to rescue him. He doesn't need to destroy the door, Brother," Tường explains, not waiting for me to finish my sentence.

Going on like this, a stroke of lightning flashes across my brain. I'm like some creature escaping from the depths of a cruel nightmare. Looking at Tường as if I'm seeing some exceptional landscape, my face blossoms.

"You, little guy, are truly a genius. It is so easy but I didn't realize it." Feeling excited, I suddenly catch myself and ask, "But her dad can't like being confined, can he?"

As soon the thought slips out, I smack my head and answer my own question almost immediately.

"Oh, I get it! No one likes to be confined and Little Plum's dad is no different. But it's because of his family, he's willing to live in the attic, that's all."

Tường gets a distant look in his eyes. "A whole life spent living in the attic, not stepping one foot to earth. Little Plum's dad has to be so miserable, don't you think?"

I pat Tường's shoulder, as if patting the worry out of his heart. "It's ok, calm down. In the middle of the night Little Plum's mom probably opens the door so her dad can go out to pee."

29.
in which I start to like Little Plum

Little Plum is surprised when I stop teasing her and calling her stupid.

Whenever we have a new homework assignment, as soon as I finish, I'll hurry over to her house and enthusiastically push my school books into her hands. "I'm done, you can copy!"

Little Plum takes the notebook, her voice emotional. "Why are you being so nice to me these days?"

I chuckle. "I've been nice to you for such a long time now! How are you so stu . . . stu . . ."

I mean to say, "How are you so stupid that you don't already know?" but I catch myself at the last moment. But Little Plum is not as stupid as I make out.

She looks at me, a smile creeping across her face. "How am I so stupid that I haven't realized it, huh?"

"I wasn't going to say that." I falter, my face reddening and my head spinning like a pinwheel to think of what kind of lie to tell. "Matter of fact . . . actually . . ."

Seeing me unhappily stumbling, Little Plum is compassionate. "You don't need to say anything more. I understand."

"What do you understand?" I clench my stomach and my eyes are stuck fast to her gentle face.

"I understand why you've been so nice to me."

Little Plum's answer is extremely vague, but her way of looking at me, deep and full of gratitude, let's me know what she is thinking.

I shyly lift my eyes up to the tree in her front yard, trying to change the subject. "This laurel tree in your front yard has a lot of fruit?"

"Yes, climb up and pick some if you want!"

"Wait until someday we're playing battle games, I'll climb up and pick some then."

The kids in my village often play this game. You only need a piece of bamboo about the length of two of your hands—we use it to create a gun and a ramrod. To fire the gun, we stuff the laurel fruits into one end of the bamboo then use the ramrod to force it out: the "bullet" shoots out with a "bump."

Getting hit with the fruit bullet doesn't hurt so much, but your shirt gets stained with blue spots. Whenever I play battle games like this, my mom will scold me when she washes my clothes.

Not knowing what else to say, I just look at Little Plum. "I'm gonna go now."

"You're going over to Beg's house, then?"

Little Plum happens to ask an ill-timed question that stops me in my tracks. Remembering the letter and that day I gave it to Little Beg, my face flames hot.

"Nope." I bite my lip, then another sentence spills out. "I'm done playing with Little Beg now."

Little Plum seems taken aback. She squints her eyes as if staring into the sun. "Why's that?"

"Not sure. Now I only like playing with you."

I don't know why I have to say that last part, because actually I'm not so clear about it. Before this, my feelings for Little Plum wouldn't fill a teaspoon of coffee.

After speaking, I'm hit with a flash of just how delicate the words are. I rub my head, embarrassed, and again look up toward the lush green of the laurel tree.

Little Plum seems deeply touched. She gently places her

hand over mine and says with sincerity, "I've liked playing with you for a long time now."

30.
the guy Sơn

The guy Sơn, Old Man Huấn's son, also likes Little Plum, though I was completely in the dark about it.

Old Man Huấn is super rich, the only one in the village who could build such a big city-style house. But the guy Sơn is a bad student, thick as a brick. Compared to him, even Little Plum is smart.

Sơn is well known for his gifts of hanging around, teasing people, breaking things, and speaking rudely. Everyone is disgusted by him.

He never even glances at his notebooks, which is why he keeps repeating one class for several years. All summers are the same: whenever the graduation ceremony comes along, we'll see his father with a whip chasing him around the village and him running in front of his father, holding his butt with both hands.

He's three years older than me and we're still in the same class.

I thought that the guy Sơn liked Little Three, Mr. Four Cang's daughter.

Little Three stopped going to school in third grade. She has stayed home since then to help her parents cut grass, sow seeds, plant rice, and spread dung every day of every month out in the sunny fields, which has turned her skin dark. And with all the hard manual labor, her body develops faster, blooming as a young lady, so that she looks even more feminine than Sister Vinh.

I don't know if Little Three actually likes the guy Sơn in return, or is just lured by his money. There's a rumor that he leads her into bushes to fool around sometimes and Mr. Four Cang has taken a machete to go after them the way someone might hunt down a dog thief.

Once I ask him, "Do you like Little Three for real?"

He crinkles his face. "I like her some. She likes me more."

"Someone said her father took his machete and went after you a bunch of times, is that right?"

The guy Sơn doesn't confirm or deny, just shrugs his shoulders. "I'm not scared of him one bit."

When he says that, it means he admits it's true. My thoughts swing back to the time Teacher Longan took his whip to go find Uncle Dan. But a whip would only hurt my uncle's body, not kill him.

"He could cut your neck with his machete and you'd be dead!" My neck reels back.

"Dead my dick, hey!" Sơn crudely pulls at his pants in the front. "If Little Three didn't cry and beg me not to, I'd have beaten her dad a long time ago!"

I don't know if Sơn is making up that part or not, but looking at his stocky wrists, I'm not sure who'd win in a fight between him and Mr. Four Cang.

The guy Sơn is about double the size of me and his hostility makes him seem always ready for a fight.

Noting my clueless face, he blinks and asks, "Have you dated Little Beg?"

I snort. "I only go over there to play capture the flag, to play the dragon and snakes game . . ."

"Stupid!" Spit sprays from his mouth. "If you like any girls, you should date them. Ask them to go behind some thick bushes where no one can see."

"No, you're stupid!" Being called out by Son, I flare up and snap back, "Go in there to be mosquito food?"

Son just shakes his head. With a bored look, he brushes his hands aside like fanning a fly. "Such a baby you are! It's boring to talk to such a stupid baby!"

"So you and Little Three go into the bushes for what?" I wet my lips, trying to compose myself.

Son smirks, disdainfully. "We play grown-up games. A baby like you couldn't understand!"

I'm at a loss for words. "What are grown-up games?"

"This game!"

Son cackles and gestures obscenely with his two hands.

"You damn pig!" I'm red in the face. "So one day Mr. Four Cang's gonna slice you into a thousand pieces!"

Then I turn around and leave.

Even after putting some distance between us, I have to stuff my fingers in my ears. Son's howling laughter follows me and sends a shiver through my whole body.

31.
a graceless demand

The guy Son admitted to me he likes Little Three.

But since I started being close to Little Plum, he can't disguise his annoyance.

In class, Little Plum and I sit at two different tables with three rows in between, but as soon as the recess bell rings, I'll immediately run out to the yard to play with her.

After capture the flag soldier edition, hopscotch, and building houses all start to get boring, the two of us will run to the schoolyard gate, put our loose change together and buy an ice cream to share, bite for bite.

When seeing that scene, the guy Sơn's eyes twitch.

One time he asks to meet me out back of the school and asks me point-blank, "Do you like Little Plum for real?"

"Yeah." I nod my head, stupefied.

"Why do you like her? I thought you liked Little Beg?"

I know why I like Little Plum. But, I can't open my mouth to speak a word of it to anyone except Tường. If the story of Little Plum's dad gets out, their shop will shut down and her family will have to go out begging.

I shudder to imagine that disaster, then give the excuse, "Little Beg turned my letter in to Teacher Longan!"

The guy Sơn eyes me suspiciously. "Just for that?"

"If I'm lying I'll eat my shoe," I say without thinking, meeting his scrutinizing eyes.

Sơn kicks up a piece of broken tile on the ground and exhales. "I'm gonna tell you now."

"What?"

"Go back to playing with Little Beg! Leave Little Plum for me." His voice is callous, as if asking for a notebook or a pair of sandals.

I have to catch my breath. "You crazy, Sơn?"

Pretending not to notice my reaction, Sơn puts a hand in his pocket and pulls out a handful of marbles. "If you agree, I'll give back these marbles."

"I'm not after any marbles."

Sơn puts his hand into another pocket. "I'll pay you."

"I don't need your damn money."

"So then I guess you need this!"

He raises his fist and scowls.

I take one step back. "So why'd you say you like Little Three?"

"I like them both," he says flatly. Then bearing his teeth, "They're both delicious to my eyes."

That terrible gesture of his from before is still a dark cloud looming in my head. As if someone has just poisoned me, my face erupts in disgust.

"Don't you dare lay your dirty hands on Little Plum!" I grind my teeth.

"You fuck off!" the guy Sơn shouts, and throws his fist at my face.

Though my guard is up, I still can't dodge that fist coming at me quick as lightning.

I fall to the floor, feeling like my jaw is shattered.

Before I have time to sit up, the guy Sơn is on top of me, punching me like he's milling grain.

I can neither punch back nor escape, just trying to cover my face with hands and elbows.

When he's had enough, Sơn pauses and says angrily, "How is it? My dirty hands on Little Plum, eh?"

Remembering her somber face and tears that day, I forget my pain.

"Your dirty fucking dog hands!" I shout and hock a gob of spit that lands right on his face with a *splat*.

The guy Sơn's bloated face immediately turns seven colors. He purses his lips and pounds my body relentlessly, not even wiping the sticky spit from his face.

As I chaotically try to shield my body, my elbow suddenly grazes something in my shirt pocket.

I blindly grab for it—a ballpoint pen—pull it out and stab it with all my might at his face.

The top of the pen makes a small dot on his cheek, perhaps not hurting him at all, which just makes his blood boil blood hotter and he beats me even more cruelly.

That day, if a friend hadn't happened to come out back to pee and threatened to tell the headmaster, perhaps my body would have been ground into sauce.

32.

in which Tường decides to get even for me

My mom is horrified when seeing me come home all roughed up with my face like a balloon.

"Oh Lord, what happened to your face?"

I lie and say that I was distracted and ran into the side of a table.

My mom quickly puts a washcloth in salt water and spreads it across my face. "Ran into the side of a table but your face is bruising on both sides?"

I pretend to breathe to get out of answering Mom's pointed questions.

The guy Tường is on the floor playing with Little Boy when I sneak to the back of the house. The fly swatter is lying beside his leg.

"You're giving him something to eat, eh?" I ask delicately.

"That's right."

Tường looks up and immediately panics. "Oh, what happened to your face?"

"Nothing happened!" I swipe my hand across my cheek, my voice trying to conceal anything dark that happened. "Just fell down is all."

"Fell?"

Tường runs his eyes across my face the way that an astronaut observes the craters of the moon, then shakes his head.

"You didn't fall!"

His gaze is still fixed on my face, and it's as if the intensity of his stare will not let me shake my head. "You fought with someone, then?"

"Yeah."

I give in, knowing that I cannot hide anything from the guy Tường. Full of sadness, I continue, "But it wasn't even fighting with someone, it was just someone hitting me."

A cloud falls over Tường's face, and I see his jaw grow more square.

"Which kid hit you, Brother?"

I hesitate for a moment then suck my teeth.

"The guy Sơn."

The guy Sơn is the most boorish in the village, all the kids are scared of him. I thought that when the name Sơn fell from my lips, a storm of fear would sweep across Tường's face.

But Tường, to my great surprise, asks, "The guy Sơn is the son of the Old Man Huấn, right?"

Then he immediately says, without letting me reply, without making any attempt to find the reason for the beating, "I will get even for you, Brother."

I am not the least bit pleased when hearing Tường declare his revenge. My heart is in a state of suspense. "And how will you get even for me?"

Tường clenches his fist. "I will hit him."

"Hitting won't do a thing." I shrug my shoulders, exhausted. "He's big like a temple pillar. You and me combined couldn't even win against him."

"Don't worry, Brother. If using strength doesn't work, then I'll use strategy."

Tường blinks while he's talking and puts a hand on my shoulder, as if to transmit one gram of his courage.

He then turns serious, giving advice exactly as if he was the older brother giving advice to the smaller one. "We can't meet him yet today. Wait until your face heals, then you can find a way to lure him out into the empty field and the two of us will beat him."

33.

in which the guy Tường takes action

I first think to lure Sơn out into the cemetery. But the cemetery is so exposed that someone might happen to see the fight. My mom, of course, would be among those who'd happen to see the scene, probably even the first audience member, as my house is right there.

After reconsidering, I decide to lure Sơn out into the grassy field behind the First Mr. Hớn's house.

The First Mr. Hớn's house, before it collapsed, which is to say, before he unfortunately had the luck of hitting the jackpot, had nothing at all around it. But when rebuilding his house, he used some pieces of the woven bamboo walls to fence in his garden and keep the pigs and chickens out.

If we fight out in that field of thick grass, surely no one will be able to see.

Persuading the guy Sơn is easy. I say, "I've been thinking about it. Let's go find some private place to talk about Little Plum," and he merrily follows right behind without an ounce of doubt.

He only suspects something is up when he sees Tường waiting there. But he's a tough guy, believes he's got superior strength to me and my brother, so he gets a bit startled but then immediately composes himself.

Sơn glowers at Tường, demanding, "What're you doing here?"

"The story of Sister Plum also concerns me."

Tường's reply is upbeat and Sơn approaches him casually, furrowing his brows. "Concerns—"

Before he can finish his sentence, Tường rushes into him and holds him in a grip.

"Hit him, Brother!" Tường shouts with his hands around Sơn's neck.

I fly into the fight, flinging punch after punch onto Sơn's spacious back, feeling as if I'm punching a wooden bed covered in buffalo leather.

After a minute of shock, the guy Sơn bears down on his hips and tries to shake Tường off. But the tiny guy has a fierce grip. Sơn staggers, then squirms around a bit but still cannot escape Tường's hold.

He finally comes up with a way to strike: rather than try to shake off the puny guy, he drops his arms down to Tường's sides.

Tường is ticklish—he screeches and immediately lets go.

To release his anger, even though I'm the one pounding his back (though my punches surely do not hurt much), Sơn seizes Tường first. He flails against Tường without restraint, growling, "Dare to sneak up on me!"

My blood boils when I see Sơn grinding his teeth and unleashing a brutal beating on my little brother's head.

I have no desire to hopelessly punch against Sơn's back anymore, so I grab his arms and try to grip them tightly. But my strength quickly drains and Sơn only has to wriggle a bit before he frees himself.

I'm not sure if Tường saw that scene or not, but he continues to scream out, "Come on, hold his arms, Brother!"

I again catch Sơn's arms and he twists away again.

On the third try I hear Sơn yelp, "Oh!" and I see him bring his hands up to cup his eyes.

"Hit him, Brother!" Tường shouts. "He can't see now!"

It happens too fast for me to understand what kind of spicy scent is in the air, but I let out a string of sneezes. It turns out that Tường put chili powder in his pants pocket, and in the moment when Sơn was distracted, he chucked a handful into his face.

It's as if Sơn is now blind, hands groping around, squealing like a sheep, eyes watering. He freaks out and turns to run away, but trips and falls over some mounds and starts thrashing about on the ground.

In the blink of an eye, me and Tường catch him while he's down. Tường sits on his legs, I mount his chest, and together we pummel him with punches.

Sơn's face by this time has paled to gray, as if just emerging from a pile of ash. Like me that day before, his hands are raised up to shield his face from punches.

Though he's scared, he has the nerve to keep threatening us. "I won't forget this, you two are gonna be so sorry."

Tường takes out from his pocket a pair of fingernail clippers. He clenches this innocent object in his palm and lets a little piece of the metal stick out. He puts it up close to Sơn, pressing it into his stomach.

"You know what this is, Sơn?"

Feeling cold metal on his belly button, Sơn's iron-hard expression starts to melt from his face. It seems he is trying to keep his teeth from chattering, but I still hear the *click-clack* in his trembling voice when he speaks. "Hey, hey . . . Don't play crazy like that, Tường!"

Tường presses the fingernail clippers a bit more. "Nothing crazy about this. You like how I play?"

Sơn is shaking ferociously, his face a chalky white now, like it's a pile of lime he's just emerged from. "Don't play stupid! If I die . . . you'll go to prison!"

Tường laughs coldly. "If I can take revenge and go to prison for it, fine with me."

"You don't have anything with me to avenge!"

"You touch my brother, you touch me, you understand?"

"Yeah . . . yeah . . ."

"Listen up so you don't forget." Tường emphasizes each

word, speaking slowly as if to let the fear really soak into Sơn's head. "From this day on, if you touch my brother, even one strand of his leg hair, I will kill you. Do you get it?"

"Yeah . . . yes . . . I get it . . . I get it . . ." Sơn continues to stammer. Perhaps he didn't expect that his star-crossed enemy would be the little guy Tường, well known in the village for his kindness.

Tường puts the fingernail clippers back into his pocket, gets up from Sơn's legs, and says to me, "Let's let him go, then."

34.
in which the guy Tường admits he's used to beatings

I praise Tường when the two of us are hustling home. "You are so good!"

"Just using some tricks."

I bite my lip. "Well, I never could've come up with such a good trick like that," I reveal. "Just seeing his bear-body lumbering toward me, my brain hardens to stone. Can't think at all!"

"Those who play up their gigantic bodies just to bully others are often pigeon-hearted." Tường speaks like a grown-up. "They're like mushy paper when meeting someone who will face them!"

I blink my eyes, admiring him. "You are so 'philosophical'!"

Tường laughs gently. "I read the sentence in a book."

"So now the guy Sơn won't dare to mess with me anymore?" I anxiously confirm. My heart is still unsettled, though I know I caught Sơn's horrified eyes as Tường was pressing the nail clippers to his belly.

Tường pats my back. "For sure. You can rest assured!"

An "ouch!" comes out of nowhere while Tường is speaking.

"What happened?" I whip around and see the little boy gingerly favoring his arm.

"No no, nothing's wrong," Tường tries to console me, though I can see him struggling not to wince. Feeling my stare, Tường lightly waves his hand away, smiling. "The pain has passed now. Just because I moved my arm suddenly, that's all."

Only now do I recall that in that horrifying fight, Tường was the only one who took a beating. He was the martyr, heading in to catch the enemy alive, sacrificing his own back. As for me, I don't think I ate a single punch!

"The pain passed? You monkey!" I scold him and feel my nose start to tickle.

"For real! The pain has passed now," Tường says, avoiding my eyes.

I kick the grass and huff. "I saw him punching you like he was grinding corn. Your bones must be like powder now!"

"Don't worry, Brother! I'm used to taking beatings."

Tường speaks with a calm voice. I'm sure he thinks he is easing my heart, but actually it makes me even more emotional. He's more handsome than me, more passionate about reading, more hardworking, more loving—everything about him is better than me. But his fate is such a misfortune. Oh, isn't there anything better he could get used to than taking beatings?!

"Why didn't you throw the chili right at the start of the fight?" I ask with regret. "So you wouldn't be corn powder!"

"How to do it from the start, Brother?" Tường shakes a thick lock of hair from his forehead. "Just seeing me, the guy Sơn was already on his guard. He was glaring at me nonstop. If I put my hands in my pockets, he would have suspected something."

I let out a sigh. "Oh, yeah."

Not knowing what more to say, I just kick the air. "You really faced him!"

35.
in which the guy Sơn is up to something again

The next day at school, I dare not approach the guy Sơn. When class starts and I have to sit right next to him, my stomach is in knots, and it stays that way for the whole morning. But from the beginning to the end of class, he sits as still as a statue.

Only when everyone takes their bags and crowds up around the gate to leave does he reach out and pat me on the back. "Hey, Thiều!"

"What's up?" I twist my body out from under his hand, wondering if Tường was wrong.

But Sơn doesn't mention our fight yesterday. He just makes a statement, a kind of riddle, nothing that warrants the anxiety I'm feeling in my gut.

"Don't assume everyone in the village is clueless."

Of course, the only reaction that materializes at that moment is gaping, as I anxiously wait to find out where that mysterious opening of his will lead.

Without making me wait for long, the guy Sơn gives a sinister scowl and his lips curl around his teeth, and he says, "You think I didn't know the secret of Little Plum's family?"

His words make me dizzy, as if someone were hammering into my head. I only want to fall to my knees.

"The fate of her family is in my hands now. She'll do everything I order her to."

His threatening voice rises and grates against my ears like salt on a wound. A heavy thing sits on my heart and my breath quickens.

"So what are you gonna do?" I ask almost breathlessly.

"What I'm gonna do, you know already." He is intentionally vague, taking pleasure in my anxiety, which is swelling from the bottom of my eyes.

In a second, I sense the blood rising hot into my face. If I could bite his neck, I wouldn't mind doing so.

I ball up my fist, and lips trembling I say, "Don't you dare touch Little Plum!"

"Hah! Is that your order, Thiều?" Sơn spits out a gob of saliva to the ground. "Who do you think you are?"

He then pats my shoulder, hissing in my ear, "Your little brother is fierce, but you're just a little mosquito to me. I could squeeze you dead with my pinky."

He then turns around and walks away, swinging his bag and singing some lines, all dirty words:

"Oh hey, baby, your boob is so round . . ."

I look around to see if Little Plum is nearby, but I don't see her.

On the other side of the fence, in the middle of the school yard, the flame tree flowers start blooming their petals to make a canopy overhead, signaling the return of summer. Cicadas hum the noisy chorus for a while. But I don't notice, consumed by the continuing saga with the guy Sơn.

So now comes the cicada-catching season. But I realize my heart is not at all relaxed. The guy Sơn's rudeness stabs into my mind and grows there like poisonous mushrooms.

Biting my lips until they bleed, I strain my neck to catch his distant figure, my eyes full of sorrow, disgust, and powerless anger, wishing hard that he'd drown in the river or burn to death.

36.

in which every day I go over to Little Plum's house

In a heavy mood and not able to share with anyone, I go around with my head in a dark cloud. Sometimes for a whole day I don't even make one sound of laughter.

Tường wonders, "What's up? Are you sad about something, Brother?"

"Nope."

I sharply dismiss his question, for such stories I know I cannot confide in Tường.

Every day I go over to Little Plum's house. There are days I go over there two, three times, just to ask her aimlessly, "Today are there any kids from our class coming over to play with you?"

Little Plum first says no, and then when I keep asking again and again the same question, she giggles and asks, "What's wrong with you, Thiều?"

I suck my teeth, confused. "Nothing's wrong with me. Just curious is all."

So the guy Sơn hasn't taken any action yet. Surely he is just waiting for the right time. I sigh and look for a smooth way to bring up this difficult subject.

"You're still air drying your fingers by the window these days?"

"Every day I air dry them, yes."

I remember her tears. "And your face? Are you still air drying your face?"

"I am."

"You're still taking beatings from your mom then, huh?"

She doesn't answer but her face sinks with sadness.

"Why does your mom often hit you?" I furrow my brows

and suddenly feel my heart tighten. "'Cause I see you working so hard at home. And your marks in school this month haven't been bad at all."

But it seems even this Little Plum doesn't want to answer. It's only when I gently touch my hand to her hand to encourage her that she falteringly replies, "My mom hits me for no reason at all. Feels an itch on her eye and hits me, that's all."

"Feels an itch on her eye? What's that?" My eyes grow round.

"I don't know either." Little Plum shakes her head, her voice beginning to get soft. "My mom just told me so."

As she speaks, Little Plum turns her head deliberately away from me. Just watching her from the back, I have the feeling that she's swallowing a sob.

Still not turning around to look at me, Little Plum continues to speak through muffled tears. "My mom is usually sad and in a bad mood."

Surely her mom is sad and in a bad mood because of the family's issues! I consider it deeply. Yes, with the status of Little Plum's father like that, her mom is surely so stressed out. She's got enough to worry about already. Worry about putting meals on the table every day for the whole family. Worry about caring for her husband. Worry about exposing secrets. Maybe it's the reason why her mom gets so irritable, hitting her for no reason at all.

I am overcome with compassion for Little Plum. I want to tell her she should watch out for the guy Son. But in the end I keep that story a secret. I don't want to upset her any more.

That day before returning home, I stand beneath the laurel tree and delicately take her hands. "Don't be sad. When your dad is better, your house will go back to being as joyful as it was before."

I say so, but I know I don't believe my words. I'm not

sure if her dad has leprosy or not, but if he does, then there's no cure. I've heard people in our village talk about it. They say the people with leprosy usually have to hide themselves in a place very far away, somewhere at the end of the forest or deep in the mountains. They live collectively with each other in a lonely world, apart from the rest of the people while waiting for Death to come and greet them. Oh, a sad story!

37.
Little Plum's attic

I wished for the guy Son's house to burn down, if he didn't fall into the river and become bait for the River Spirit first.

But the house that burned down was Little Plum's.

It was our last class before the end of the school year. Actually, we just go to class for the party.

On this day, everyone hauls their desks around to form a big triangle, rearranging the space to display the candy, fruits, and soda that we'll eat and drink before playing around and finishing the class with songs—which basically means a screaming and clapping competition. Once we're full of food and singing, the whole group runs outside to watch the kite-flying show of all the classes.

While Little Plum and I are captivated by the colorful kites meandering through the sky, the son of Old Mr. Five Bottles, Chair, appears from out of nowhere and stops his bicycle beside the fence. He directs his voice into the school-yard with an urgent cry. "Hey, Sister Plum! Your house is burning! Hurry home!"

Little Plum's face drains of all color and she runs like the wind through the gate, as if she was flying over the earth.

I instantly follow, running behind her and looking around

in bewilderment, my heart aching with every step.

The guy Chair waits with his bike for Little Plum to come bursting out from the gate, and I race to keep up with them on foot.

I hear the sound of thumping feet behind me and when I turn back around, I see a group of five other kids on my tail. They're the ones who were standing nearby and heard what was going on. And now, just out of curiosity, they are coming to see—as if they're going to a feast and not to a burning house.

By the time I arrive, the flames have mostly been smothered. The neighbors are huddled around and murmuring among themselves. People are carrying buckets of water, people are carrying pots of water, people are cupping water in their hands. I even see my mom and the guy Tường standing there confounded, their clothes dirty and dishevelled, looking pathetic.

I don't see Little Plum anywhere. I sneak around to the back of the house, then onto the veranda, trying not to run into my mom.

The attic in the back has been completely consumed by flames. Clouds of black smoke hover in the air. Little Plum and her mom and a few others are busy digging in the ground, salvaging things from the fire's wreckage. The mother and daughter are hunched over, combing through the ashes and crying at the same time.

I hide behind a banana tree, and faintly exhale: thank Luck, if people hadn't come in time, surely the flames would've spread and Little Plum's property would have been transformed into ash right before our eyes.

My exhalation is cut short—I remember Little Plum's dad. I gasp to think of Little Plum's dad confined up in the attic. I don't know if he was able to get out or not. Her mom is such a wreck now, maybe something happened to her dad. My stomach tightens as I envision the gentle and thin man who cut my hair for so many years of my childhood, and tears well up in my eyes.

A hand is placed on top of my hand and a voice speaks softly but sternly, "Go on home, Son."

I pull back. "Mom, I want to see Little Plum. I want to see if . . ."

"You can see her another day. This isn't a place for kids."

As my mom says this, she drags me out of the gate with the guy Tường slumping along behind.

38.
an orphaned little bird

Little Plum's mom was arrested that afternoon.

The county police stated that they found human bones in the fire, so they had to take her mother in to investigate.

The story that Little Plum's dad had been secretly living in the attic spreads across the village like wildfire.

That afternoon, everywhere I go I only hear people talking about it, in all kinds of tones, some mourning, some blaming, some lamenting, some pitying.

The adults discuss it nonstop while the kids swarm like flies around them trying to overhear the stories. I alone am away from the crowds. Seeing others spreading rumors about Little Plum's family disturbs me deeply, as if I myself am being preyed upon by them.

I wander around for the whole afternoon. When darkness settles in, feeling so anxious, I have to sprint to Little Plum's house.

The scene of her house is still chaotically disordered, smoke still hanging in the air. Seems Little Plum didn't want to clean anything. When I get there, she's sitting on the front doorstep, her head collapsed into her hands as if it might never lift up again. It seems she hasn't stirred from this position since noon.

My heart melts in that moment, feeling the unmistakably miserable look on my dear friend's face, the look of one who's suddenly been defeated by a blink of fate.

Not wanting to startle her, I stand still under the laurel tree and quietly watch her. It seems she's no more than an orphaned newborn bird.

Just in one day, her house burned, her father died, her mom went to jail. It's like the whole of hell just crashed down on her head.

I hear rustling sounds inside the house, then my mom appears. I guess she's helping with the house cleaning and rearranging.

Mom recognizes me as soon as she steps out.

I watch her back, anxiously waiting to see what she'll do, but contrary to my expectations, she doesn't shoo me away.

My mom just says gently, as if without thinking, with exhaustion carved into her face, "Is that Thiều, ah?"

She asks as if she doesn't see me, or she sees me but isn't sure who I am.

"Yes, Mom," I mumble.

Then she does shoo me away.

"Go on home, dear. Having me here to clean is enough."

My heart sinks. But before I can open my mouth to protest, she continues, "Go on home to eat and take a bath first, then you can come back over later this evening to sleep here, help take care of the house for your friend."

"Yes, Mom."

I happily nod my head, completely surprised by my mom's request.

In that feeling of strange elation, I glance over at Little Plum, but she seems unaware of the conversation between me and Mom.

She sits there, with her head still sorrowfully collapsed in her arms, with her hair strewn across one shoulder, withdrawn into the gray night of herself, a lonely statue sculpted by sadness and placed in front of her house ages ago.

39.
the evening at Little Plum's house

That evening, I bring Little Plum a tin of rice with some fried shrimp.

She's not any less withered, but does seem to brighten a bit when seeing me.

"Are you coming to sleep here and look after the house with me, Thiều?"

It means she heard my mom's suggestion that afternoon when sitting on the doorstep.

I "uhmhm" and put the tin on the table.

"My mom told me to bring you some food. Have you had dinner yet?"

"I don't want to eat anything." Her voice is almost a whisper.

"You should eat something to stay healthy." I repeat the words Mom often tells me when I'm lazy to eat.

Little Plum's stubborn. "But I'm not hungry."

My eyes float off to the side while I'm thinking of at least one good reason.

"Your mom would be sad if she knew you didn't eat."

I bring up her mom to convince her to eat out of her devotion, but she just bursts into tears.

"How to know when my mom will be released?"

"I'm sure it'll be soon."

I just answer for the sake of answering, though my gut says that if the police discover her mom was confining her dad in the attic and he accidently died in the fire, perhaps it will take a long time for her to be released.

Maybe Little Plum shares the same thought, because she doesn't show any relief at my attempt to console. She keeps weeping for a bit then put her hands on her chin, looking out at the sky without any life in her eyes. For a moment I feel her mind and heart wandering somewhere very far away, perhaps the place where the sun is going to bed.

I don't know what kind of images are looming in Little Plum's head, but I feel sorry for her when seeing the way she sits there.

I click my tongue, just to break the suffocated air. "But how'd the attic catch fire and burn, do you know, Plum? No one cooks up there. And your dad didn't smoke at all."

Little Plum turns around and looks at me, bewildered for some time, then finally seems to get the sense of what I said.

"Perhaps my dad was careless." She weeps. "In the attic, there's an oil lamp near the Buddha statue."

"I see."

I nod my head and casually say, while pushing out my chair to stand up, "Let me go get you a bowl and chopsticks for your rice, then."

"I can just eat with the tin. Don't need a bowl and sticks."

I have a private field day when seeing Little Plum go along. She no longer wants to insist on suffering hunger.

"So I will go get a spoon for you, then." I run as quickly as possible to the kitchen.

40.

Little Plum's house at night

Little Plum's house has two bamboo beds.

At night, I sleep on the bed in the room outside of where she's been sleeping, beside a rickety desk. She sleeps on her mom's bed.

Her mom's bed is in the inner room, beside the shelves holding fish sauce, soy sauce, dried noodles, and assorted spices.

Of course, I am overjoyed when my mom sends me out to sleep at Little Plum's house. I don't really know what I can do to help her at this time, just be there to ease her fear of burglars, fear of ghosts. That's all I can do.

Though I am the master of being afraid of ghosts, Little Plum's unlucky situation has made me so emotional that I completely forget my own fear.

Only when darkness descends, when Little Plum goes into her room to lie down, when there's just one oil lamp flickering at the top of the cabinet, do I begin to tremble. The buzzing of insects echoes in from the cemetery. At home I never notice it, but tonight the distinct sound surprises me. That monotonous sound steadily scratches at my heart, making it clench up every time.

My thoughts wander back to Little Plum's dad. Meeting his untimely death just today at noon, surely his soul's ghost is flying somewhere around here now. Perhaps standing beside my bed and I just don't see it.

The more I think, the more scared I get. I pull the blankets up around my head but it doesn't calm my fears in the slightest. I kick myself for not letting the guy Tường come along. If he were lying beside me, surely I wouldn't be so frightfully numb as I am now.

Fear spreads its claws and seizes me completely when I

feel the bed wiggle. And when I recognize that there's definitely someone sitting there on the bed, right beside me, my jaw freezes stiff, my throat tries to scream out loudly, but only a spray of meaningless sounds comes out.

"Don't be scared, Thiều. It's me!"

Little Plum knows very well that I'm freaking out, and her voice is delicate. Lying down beside me, she continues, "I'm really scared sleeping in that room alone."

Realizing it's Little Plum and not her dad, my racing heart gradually slows down. Turns out Little Plum is a scaredy-cat like me. She's always slept with her mom and dad. Tonight's the first night of sleeping by herself, and surely after such a radical change she is anxious and disturbed.

I scoot over and peep my head out of the blanket. I confess a bit gleefully, "For a moment I was also super scared, tossing and turning around. But having you beside me now, I can be calm enough to get some sleep."

Little Plum is a girl, she runs over to sleep beside me in the middle of the night—surely she must be embarrassed. Even though I'm chatty, she doesn't say anything. I am about to blabber some more sentences but I see that she's distracted and looking off somewhere else, so I keep silent.

That night, before falling asleep, I see her holding a pillow between us. Girls are horribly cautious!

41.

in which I meet Uncle Dan in the morning

Little Plum's idea of holding a pillow between us is to make a barrier. She's afraid that in the middle of the night while lost in sleep, she'll roll over to my side or I'll roll over to her side. And this would be absolutely mortifying.

But Little Plum's barrier doesn't block anything. By the morning, I open my eyes to see that she's thrown her arm around both the pillow and me. Still sleeping, her gentle breath flutters the hair scattered across her rosy cheek.

I watch her closed eyes, the few teardrops that still haven't dried on her face. She must have been crying all night. I feel emotional and carefully move her arm off of me.

I gaze at her for a bit longer then tiptoe gingerly out of the house.

I meet Uncle Dan on the road home.

"You woke up early, eh?" He squints to look at me.

"Last night I slept at Little Plum's house. Mom told me to stay overnight to be there for her."

"Ah yes, good to help your friend." Uncle Dan pats my head with his only hand.

I don't know why but at that time I remember Little Plum's fingers in bloom. "Hey, Uncle. Little Plum's got ten fingers in bloom!"

"Oh, really?" Uncle Dan laughs. "Your friend probably writes and draws quite beautifully, then!"

I know that Little Plum writes and draws not even a tiny bit beautifully. But I don't dispute Uncle Dan's claims. Maybe because Little Plum spends all her time with house-work, she can't practice writing and drawing like the other kids. If she could have the kind of free time that I have, no doubt she'd be the best in the class.

Out of the blue I say, "I'm scared of ghosts but Little Plum is even more scared of them than me. In the middle of the night last night she was clutching a pillow and ran over to sleep in the bed with me."

Immediately fearing a misunderstanding, I quickly follow up with, "Little Plum placed a pillow between her and me."

Uncle Dan stifles a laugh. "And so then what?"

"So then we slept, Uncle," I innocently reply. "With her lying beside me, my fear just disappeared. I slept like a log!"

Uncle Dan gives me a look. "Going over to help a friend and sleeping so deeply like that, someone's able to come in and steal you away."

"Don't worry, Uncle." I laugh. "This morning I felt her hugging me so tightly, no way a burglar could steal me away."

As soon as that comes out of my mouth, I unexpectedly blush. I feel annoyed with myself for having rashly told Uncle Dan some details I shouldn't share with just anyone.

But Uncle Dan's reaction is not what I expect. His voice abruptly lowers, seemingly thoughtful. "Your friend isn't afraid of ghosts at all. Your friend is afraid of emptiness. You should stay by her side, ok?"

42.

in which I meet the guy Sơn at noon

I don't know how the guy Sơn knows I slept at Little Plum's house last night.

Perhaps he saw me taking the tin to Little Plum's house or going out from there in the morning.

At noon, while I'm walking with the tin on the road, the guy Sơn falls into step with me. "You're bringing food for Little Plum, right?"

Feeling protective, I answer with a question. "How do you know?"

"What don't I know!" Sơn curls his lips. "I even know that you slept at her house last night!"

I startle, a sudden insecurity takes over. The fire at Little Plum's house also accidently burned Sơn's ugly scheme to ashes. The story of Little Plum's dad is now out in the open, he no longer has anything to threaten her with. Maybe for that, he's angry with envy, looking for ways to talk bad about my friend.

I steel my stomach against worrying and hastily explain, "My mom told me to go over and help her look after the house."

"Hah, look after the house!" Sơn snickers and assumes his disrespectful tone. "So you're not going over there to sleep with her and make this, hah?"

The guy Sơn makes a swirling gesture with his fingers to shock me.

"Curse you!" My face grows pale. "I'm not the kind of dog you are!"

I grip the handle of the tin in anger and walk away. If I didn't think Little Plum was hungry now, I would whop the tin across the guy Sơn's head.

His cackling voice is still behind me. "If you don't know what to do, then lemme go over and look after her house tonight!"

I'm so furious that my face is still a pale stone even by the time I get to Plum's house.

She quickly recognizes the strange look on my face. "What's wrong with you, Thiều?"

I lie. "Nothing's wrong at all. Just worrying that you'd be hungry so I tried to run as hard as possible." I catch my breath and continue. "Tonight you should find some logs and put them on the front bed, ok?"

"For what?" She's confused.

"To protect yourself." I press my lips together tightly. "Just in case there's any evening I can't come over, if a burglar enters your house, you have the weapons for defense."

Little Plum doesn't know that as I am saying this my head is spinning with the image of Sơn. She promptly nods her head. "You are so caring, Thiều! I never thought of that."

43.

in which Little Plum stays at my house

My defense strategy turns out not to be necessary.

In the early afternoon, my mom goes to visit Little Plum's mom at the county jail. When she's back, she tells Little Plum to pack up her clothes and books to come stay at our house.

As for their house, Little Plum's mom asks my mom to help sell it.

My mom sends me to find a thin piece of tin on which I can paint the words HOUSE FOR SALE then hang it out in the front of the house, where her dad's HAIR STYLE sign used to be.

"For people in our village, the board isn't necessary," my mom says. "But now those passing through will see it and know."

Little Plum follows my mom to our house, half-sad and half-relieved. Sad to leave her home, relieved to not live all by herself in that deserted house anymore. The status of her heart seems quite complicated, but I can understand the feelings that are tormenting her. "Half-sad, half-relieved" is just a familiar saying, and I guess that when stepping out of her house, Little Plum's heart was carrying ninety percent sadness.

I know I'd be the same way if, for some reason, I was forced to leave my childhood home where I've spent my whole life, where I know every broken brick by heart, every termite nest in the back garden, even know by heart every spot where sunlight pierces through the thatched roof and brings the flowers to bloom in the summer. I know my heart would be ripped to shreds.

My mom and Little Plum clasp the clothes and books while I lug the wobbly desk behind them.

On the way, my mom is the only one to try consoling Little Plum. She walks beside my mom, just nodding and saying yes, sometimes wiping away her tears.

I bring the desk to my house in silence, partly because the carrying gets heavier and heavier, partly because I don't know what words to open with.

After puzzling over where to set up the desk for Little Plum, eventually finding a spot near the window in between the dining table and the few bags of cement my dad bought as foundation for a well, I suddenly remember something to ask.

"Oh, so where's your dog Vện, Plum? Why didn't you bring him here too?"

Little Plum's eyelids close. "He's dead."

"When'd he die?" I scratch my head, feeling uneasy. "So that's why I haven't seen him for several days."

"Last week."

"Poor guy." I click my tongue, then, afraid that'll sadden her even more, I add with a light snort, "Though he was so old already."

The dog Vện was with Plum's family for a long time. From the time I was just a tiny kid, I'd always see him romping around Little Plum everywhere she went. To calculate his age, perhaps he was the same age as she. The average age of a dog is around ten years. Vện had lived so long already. His eyes were almost blind, his movements so slow and rickety, his hair more and more scruffy. Every time I went over to Plum's house, I'd see him lying motionless under the bed, as if waiting for death.

But Vện shouldn't have died now, not at this miserable time for Little Plum's family and their house. The thought wrenches my insides: even the dog has left Little Plum behind!

44.

in which Mr. Four Cang goes after the guy Sơn

Little Plum is a year older than me but she still acts like a little kid.

Little kids don't know how to nurture and prolong their sadness as enduringly as grown-ups do.

After a few days at my house, Little Plum starts to remember how to smile.

The guy Tường really takes to Little Plum. She is a responsible kid, hands always busy with some work. Since her arrival at our house, Tường's got a much lighter load of chores.

When having free time, Tường invites Little Plum to go catch flies. The two of them go around together for the whole afternoon before playing with Little Boy toad under the bed.

After having their fill of Little Boy, the two of them pull some books from the shelf and go out to sit by the well, reading and giggling together.

To watch Tường and Little Plum, I sense that it's often the case that kids who aren't so good in school can get along easily together. But I should leave them be. If Little Plum is happy, then I'm happy.

Around then, I receive some very good news. I overhear someone in the village gossiping about how Mr. Four Cang rode his buffalo on a rampage after the guy Sơn, chasing him all the way out to Clay Field.

Sơn was messing around with Little Three in the bushes again and Mr. Four Cang caught them. Mr. Four Cang was just taking the buffalo out to bathe, so he didn't have his machete to cut the guy's head off.

In a fit of cosmic anger, Mr. Four Cang leapt onto the back of his buffalo and started screaming and slapping it to stay hot on Sơn's tracks, just like Guan Yunchang riding his horse Red Hare out of battle.

As soon as Sơn saw the two curved horns of the buffalo, sharp as knives and rushing toward him, he got scared out of his mind and let go of Little Three, with just enough time to start bolting for his life.

From behind, Mr. Four Cang was determined not to let Sơn get away and nimbly steered the buffalo to stay right on his heels. In front, Sơn was running and wailing for help. The buffalo's pounding feet, Mr. Four Cang's bellowing, and the ceaseless rattling of the buffalo's ding-donging neck bells combined to scare the soul out of Sơn.

The neighbors in the village poured out in droves to watch, but nobody could come up with a way to rescue Sơn. Mr. Four Cang's vehicular buffalo had let loose like the wind, with its fiery eyes flashing in a rage, its mouth foaming like a crazed animal. If anyone was caught in its path, it could've pierced through their guts like nothing.

At last someone thought of a wonderful trick. "Up the tree! Climb up the tree right away!"

In the end, Sơn was able to hustle up a mangosteen tree growing in the field, his clothes tattered, his nose and ears full of dust. He sat up in the tree, his arms and legs still fiercely trembling, his face completely drained of blood, his mouth in a crooked line, wanting so badly to cry but not crying.

That day, when Old Man Huấn heard the news, he sped off to defend his son. But out of fear of the crazed buffalo, he only dared to stand back at a distance and call out curses.

For half an hour, Mr. Four Cang and Old Man Huấn exchanged curses back and forth until it seemed everyone's ears were bleeding. There came a time when the villagers who were gathered around finally succeed in convincing Mr.

Four Cang to curb his anger. Still furious, he directed the buffalo away toward the Lồ Ồ Stream.

I didn't witness this drama with my own eyes—I only heard about it from friends later—but I am pleased for a whole week. It's just a pity that my dad was out working far away. I'm sure if he were home, he would've made up a rhyme that divulged what the guy Sơn had done, and it'd be spread widely around the village among all the kids and neighbors so Old Man Huấn and the guy Sơn would never dare to show their faces again.

I tell the story about Sơn to Tường and Little Plum. Tường retracts his neck. "That's so scary!"

Little Plum screws up her face. "In the bushes there's nothing at all. Why would Sơn bring Little Three there just to put Mr. Four Cang into a blind rage?"

45.
Little Plum's happy news

The story of Sơn narrowly escaping death by Mr. Four Cang's buffalo is happy news only to me.

Tường and Little Plum receive the news in an unaffected way, barely curious at all. Little Plum doesn't know that Sơn ever had shadowy plans for her too. And the same goes for Tường. After scaring Sơn shitless, he sees it as justice restored and isn't the least bit concerned with that ogre anymore.

The news that all three of us can celebrate is the news my mom brought from the county police station.

I can read it immediately on my mom's glowing face, fresh with happiness, when she steps through the door carrying some baskets.

"Plum! Hey, Plum!" Mom plops down into a chair, unfastens her conical hat, and uses it to fan herself, her face bubbling.

"Yes?" Little Plum dashes out excitedly, as if she has a premonition that whatever my mom is about to say is extremely important to her.

"Your mom will soon be released."

It's like a bomb goes off: me, Little Plum, and Tường explode in cheers and start jumping around.

"Oh, it's true?!" Little Plum is almost screaming, and she needs to put her hand on the table to brace herself.

"It's true. I heard the police saying that the bones they found in the attic were not human bones."

"Not human bones? So, my dad is still alive?" Little Plum's voice is shaking as she asks, jubilant, innocent, tearful.

"Yeah." My mom nods her head. "If the bones they found weren't human bones, then your dad is surely still alive."

"So where is he?"

Little Plum's round eyes look at my mom, as if really believing my mom could answer that.

"That I don't know."

My mom sighs and is quiet for a moment. Then she resumes her joyful tone while carrying the bags from the market into the kitchen. "So if your dad is still alive, that means you'll meet him again sooner or later."

I have a line of questions forming in my head but try to force my lips to stay sealed. Little Plum is overjoyed, and I don't want to interrupt her emotions at all.

I only open my mouth when my mom is no longer there. "Hey, Plum."

"What is up, Thiều?" Little Plum turns to look at me with her glistening eyes and bright face.

I scratch the back of my neck. "You know your dog, Vện?"

"What about Vện?"

"You said he died a week ago, right?"

"Yeah."

"And so what did you do with his corpse?"

"I buried him in the banana trees out behind the veranda."

After saying this, Little Plum's eyes get wide in wonder. "Why are you asking?"

I swallow. "I suppose that Vện's corpse isn't there anymore."

46.
the dog's corpse

And just as I supposed, when the three of us bring shovels to Plum's garden and set about digging up the earth where the dog was buried, we find no corpse at all.

Tường pauses his digging, wipes the sweat from his forehead, and asks, "Are you sure this is the right place, Sister Plum?"

"Yes, right here," Little Plum states. "Just dig a bit deeper!"

"Enough digging, already." I balk when seeing Tường raise his shovel again. "There's no Vện under the ground here at all, I'm sure!"

Little Plum glares at me. "So you know where his corpse is then, Thiều?"

I hesitate for a moment then it bursts out of me, the doubt that's been clinging to my mind since my mom said Little Plum's dad was still alive.

"I think the bones they collected the other day from the attic are Vện's."

"How could they be Vện's bones?" Little Plum is flustered.

Unlike Little Plum, Tường is able to read my mind in

a second. "You mean Sister Plum's dad secretly took the corpse up to the attic, Brother?"

"Umhm." I exhale strongly. "And if I'm right, that means the fire was caused by Plum's dad, on purpose."

"But why would he do that? He . . . burning his own house down?" Little Plum sputters, bewildered. She seems about to faint. Perhaps the image of the burning house has stabbed a hole in her heart.

I bite my lower lip. "Maybe your dad wanted to flee, so he wouldn't be a burden on your family anymore?"

"But why would he do it like that?" Little Plum starts to blink her reddening eyes. "If he wanted to flee, why not just leave, why burn the house?"

"Yeah," Tường adds, "because if the neighbors hadn't come in time that day, the whole house would've burned to ash!"

I just keep rubbing my nose, frowning, thinking.

"I think your dad planned everything out beforehand." I glance at Little Plum, shake my head, and keep talking. "Maybe before starting the fire, he watered the rest of the house so the flames wouldn't spread. He was the only one home that day, right?"

"Yeah."

My hand moves up my face and knocks on my forehead. "Or, maybe because the attic's the highest part of the house, your dad thought that when the flames rose, the neighbors would run over and put them out before they spread to the lower part."

Little Plum gives another "yeah," but her eyes are so bewildered that it frightens me. I don't know if she even heard what I said.

"But if he was home alone that day, why wouldn't he just quietly leave, Brother?" The question from Tường is exactly the same as the question Little Plum asked before.

"Yeah, why didn't my dad just quietly walk out?" Little Plum mechanically repeats after Tường.

I forcefully sigh. "If your dad had just quietly left, you and your mom would've definitely gone looking for him as soon as you found out. So he had to create a scene of fire as a distraction. But because that still wasn't the most secure way, worrying that people would know he escaped, he secretly moved Vện's corpse up to the attic so everyone would think the bones were his . . ."

Little Plum puts a hand to her chest.

"So what if my mom has to go to prison for this?"

"How would she? The police just have to look at those bones to know they're from a dog. I think your dad knew she'd only be detained a few days for them to investigate."

I continue while turning my back to get to the gate, "At least that's probably what he hoped. So that when she was released, he'd be far away."

47.
Little Plum and the guy Tường

Tường has always been an unconditional admirer of mine. Now, after listening to me lecture about why Little Plum's father burned the attic, it seems like he wants to kneel before me.

Following me, praising me nonstop: "Brother, you are so intelligent!" "You're going to become a minister of the government when you grow up!"

Tường doesn't know what a minister does, but in his imagination, it must be a very important job.

I flare my nostrils. "Just the other day you were saying I'll become a general!"

"You can be a general when having wars. But if you're not going to the battlefield, Brother, you'll be a minister."

He raises his pinky and looks at me. "You want to bet on it, Brother?"

"Enough." I brush my hand through the air. "I'll only bet on something that's happening before my eyes. Betting on being a minister is such a distant thing, just have to wait until it happens."

Tường is happy, Little Plum is also happy. Since learning that her dad is still alive and her mom is going to be released soon, Little Plum seems like another person, smiling and talking all the time, completely unlike the previous image of a sentimental Plum.

But actually, Little Plum's mom isn't being released immediately. Though she's not charged with involuntary manslaughter, the county officials still continue to investigate the crime of confining her husband in the attic, even though everyone knows now that he could have escaped whenever he wanted.

Little Plum has also been called into the station to be questioned about the situation. Each time she comes back, her eyes are twinkling with some hope when I ask her about it.

"My mom's gonna be free soon, I'm sure. I told them my dad voluntarily let my mom keep him up in the attic, he wasn't forced!"

When she says this, Little Plum's face shines like an early morning sunbath and I can't possibly pull my eyes away. In those moments, she becomes a kind of flower that I'm watching. Feeling her joy gently enter my soul, unmistakably, I can recognize my own joyful face illuminated in her eyes.

If there's any twinge to this joy, it's that whenever Little Plum's done responding to my first question, she'll promptly speed off to find the guy Tường before I can ask a second question. Later, if I wander around the back yard, without fail I'll meet the two of them working on something. Either they're sweeping with the areca brooms, or lugging a bag of grain over to Lady Thoan to grind powder for my mom's rice cakes, or paying attention to something else, but always together.

48.
the thorn in my side

Tường and Little Plum share a lot of things in common that I don't.

I don't enjoy being a busy bee with constant housework. I don't carry out burdensome tasks with lighthearted jokes like they do. I don't enjoy silly, childish games like plucking leaves, gathering tin cans to play shop, or hunting for dwarf ylang-ylang flowers just to pick and pocket them for the smell. And lastly, I cannot imagine being one of those people who can plant their face inside the pages of a book filled with words, hour after hour, or plaster myself beside a bed all day playing with a toad.

With similar personalities, it's understandable that they'd be stuck together all the time. But even with this in mind, I don't understand why, I still feel annoyed.

Before moving to our house, I remember clearly how Little Plum murmured, "I've liked playing with you for a long time now," and how in her loneliest hour she hugged me tightly while sleeping.

And yet, it would seem now that Little Plum remembers nothing of that. It feels bitter and sad to realize that when she was staying in her house and I in my house, the two of us seemed closer than when we share one house.

Now, it's like two worlds inside one house: while I spend the whole day inside or running around the front yard, Little Plum and Tường are cooing softly in the back yard.

Of course the guy Tường loves me. Every day he begs me, "Hey, brother, come out and play with me and Sister Plum!"

Sometimes it's possible for me to play with them, but I get bored pretty quickly, just carrying buckets of water back and forth between the well and the big jar by the kitchen several times until our arms are dead tired. As soon as we stop to rest, they'll pull out a matchbox with a click beetle inside to start playing with, gesturing for me to join, but I don't feel at all interested. Honestly it seems absurd to me, lying and crawling on the ground for a whole hour just listening to the faint and monotonous buzz of click beetles whirring their tails.

But what annoys me most is how I don't have the chance to tell Little Plum things like "Now I only like playing with you" or "Are you still air drying your fingers outside the window these days?"

With the guy Tường right there, I can only ask Little Plum tedious things like "You're not going to cover your head all day out in the sun?" or "Have you finished sweeping the floor yet?" and this saddens me deeply.

There are times I stubbornly try to sabotage their playing. I stick my head out the door and scream at the top of my lungs, "Hey, Tường, what are you up to?!"

"Me and Sister Plum are catching worms. Come out and catch them with us!"

The worms are tiny as seeds, often digging in rows through the sand or dirt. Wherever the worms are nestled, the surface of the ground rises in swirls like the mouth of a little funnel. When discovering one, kids will usually hunch down and purse their lips to gently blow the sand up. After a while, the worm will come out. Like someone who was fast asleep then got their blankets ripped off, the worm abruptly wakes up and spins around in all directions before nestling back into the sand to . . . keep sleeping. Two or three years ago, I was still interested in this game. Whoever could find the biggest one of all the worm caves was the winner. But now I feel the game is boring.

"I don't want to play that. Can you come here and help me with something?"

And so Tường gives up the game and dashes away.

The story of me needing Tường's help is, of course, nonsense. I either make up some trivial task for him, or ask him to do something I could easily do myself. For example, "Help me find the eraser!" or, "Go get a handful of rice from the kitchen for me so I can stick a label to my notebook!"

Tường is always happy to help me. He goes off to search for a rubber eraser or some leftover rice with a smile on his face. My little brother is innocent, not protesting the ridiculous requests, not considering for one second that I'm deliberately playing some mean trick on him.

49.
an ugly status of heart

My mood grows increasingly perturbed.

The image of intimacy between Tường and Little Plum haunts me, even in sleep. In all honesty, I often wish there was something else to think about these days so I wouldn't constantly think about them, but I'm totally helpless. It's painful to realize something's been nailed into my mind and will stay stuck deep in there, without any way to spit it out.

Every morning, Little Plum wakes up and seems to look a bit more charming than the day before and it utterly breaks me. What's even more heartbreaking is how I'm starting to pay more attention to Tường's appearance.

Before this, I always knew my little brother was handsome, but it was something that would casually occur to me and then immediately be forgotten. Just like I knew we had a beautiful wardrobe or a beautiful table and chair set in my house. I was excited when we first brought them home and then gradually I got used to seeing them and they became quite normal, not as interesting as before. But now, I catch myself secretly observing Tường many times a day, and each time I watch him, I discover just a bit more of his beauty, which makes my life more miserable.

The bad mood stings even more because I know very well that Tường is still an innocent kid and Little Plum just sees him as a younger brother.

It seems these days that I'm lost between confusing emotions, every day going gradually deeper down a narrow and dark path of feelings. I am vaguely aware of being stuck between jealousy and anger without cause, but not knowing any way to escape.

Since that day I learned about the guy Sơn's ugly intentions toward Little Plum, and learning the depth of my hatred for him, I have realized I'm not a kid anymore. There is something that creeps into my heart when I think about her. Gradually, I feel indifferent one tiny bit at a time, and I feel indifferent to the games that used to fascinate me—games that Little Plum and Tường are presently playing and I am refusing.

There are usually three people I can vent my feelings to: Tường, Little Plum, and Uncle Dan. But I can't vent to any of them about this and it makes my brain truly heavy.

It's a time now that I have to play two roles in life: the intense prosecutor to condemn Tường and Little Plum, and the emphatic lawyer to defend them. And so my mind is always fluctuating, my heart very much like a pendulum swinging back and forth between two extremes. In the end my heart is even more mixed up than a person jumping back and forth between tubs of hot and cold water. As you probably know (because you must have also experienced this), the heart is feverish and there is not a single cure.

I am both in agony over Tường and Little Plum's closeness, and also in agony over my agonizing: the two torments are superimposed on each other and give me the sense that I'm drowning.

And in this time of drowning in wretched emotions, I do something that will forever stay deeply in me as a regret.

50.
the story of ghost devils

It's a day that several accidental occurences happen all at once. If even just one of those occurrences didn't happen, then the ghost devils wouldn't have written this story.

The most significant occurrence of the day is that both Little Plum and the guy Tường are away: in the early morning the two set out with a bag of rice to grind at Lady Thoan's place.

The second occurrence is that Mr. Five Bottles, Chair's father, came over to my house looking for my dad. My dad was not yet back from working in the city, and my mom was not home.

The third occurrence is that the boy Melon, Old Mr. Five Bottles' son, Chair's younger brother, has rickets. Melon is twelve years old, the same age as Tường, but he looks only eight or nine, always teased and bullied for being small.

Having heard someone say that toad meat cures rickets, Old Mr. Five Bottles wanders all along the river banks and throughout the fields to catch toads to nourish his thin son.

When he comes over to my house, it's only me there. I'm sitting at my desk drawing nonsense with the pack of colored pencils I was rewarded with at the end of the school year. He enters.

"Is your dad back this month, dear?"

"No, he's not, Uncle."

"And where's your mom?"

"My mom's also out now, Uncle."

I don't know why Old Mr. Five Bottles is looking for my father. After asking a series of questions, he walks around the house then scurries into the back room while asking, "Do you know if there's a kettle to cook medicine here?"

"No, sorry Uncle, I don't know," I answer, guessing that Mr. Xung gave him medicine for the boy Melon, and follow him to the back room.

Old Mr. Five Bottles' eyes are attentive, perhaps just eager to find a kettle. Scanning the room, he catches sight of Little Boy squatting under the bed, sleeping in his cave. Perhaps when hearing someone's steps, it thinks the guy Tường is about to feed it and so it jumps out to the foot of the bed, eyes lifted in anticipation.

"Oh, a toad!" Old Mr. Five Bottles shouts out.

"Yeah."

The word rolls out of my mouth. I was about to say "It's the Little Boy of Tường," but I end up holding my tongue.

Recalling how Tường and Little Plum have giggled together for hours on end in front of the bed while playing with Little Boy, my face flushes hot. Of course I know what Old Mr. Five Bottles is going to do with the toad, but I'm blinded by jealousy.

I decide to bind my mouth shut with an invisible clip when Old Mr. Five Bottles says joyfully, "Oh, this toad just hopped in out of nowhere! Lemme catch it for my boy Melon, then!"

He bends down, and his skillful hands easily envelope Little Boy, who just sits there, not knowing what's occurring.

51.
Tường's sadness

To tell the truth, when Old Mr. Five Bottles reached down, I shut my eyes. I didn't see how he caught Little Boy, but I still quiver to imagine it as his fingers grabbing my heart.

I am both celebratory and ashamed of celebrating. When he said, "I'll head home now, bye!" I nodded with half-closed eyes, wanting to shout, "Uncle, it's actually my brother's toad! Please leave it!" But the latent jealous anger has been accumulating for so long in my heart that it turned into a dam, blocking my throat. The only utterance that came out was just some nonsensical sounds of "uh" and "uhm."

It is precisely noon when the guy Tường discovers Little Boy's missing.

He and Little Plum anxiously go around the house, scouring the dark corners and continuously calling the toad's name.

After a while, Tường runs out to the front yard where I'm pretending to play marbles by myself. He grips my shoulder and is almost in tears. "Have you seen Little Boy, Brother?"

"Your toad, uh?" I raise my eyes, and speaking in my most measured voice I say, "I just saw it around here earlier!"

"But now he's gone!" Tường can't stop crying.

I look away. "I think it's just under the bed!"

"No, nothing's there, Brother. I called him 'til I was blue in the face and still he's not coming out like he always does."

Tường is weeping and shaking my shoulders, the way I often see the sickest villagers asking Mr. Xung for help.

I hypothesize, "Or it's just sleeping so deeply?"

At these words, Tường tears back to the house in a flash. This time, he and Little Plum struggle to move the bed a little, then the two of them take an oil lamp to search every inch of the ground. Hunched over, their mouths almost touching the ground, they're straining to see the toad's cave and screaming its name until my ears hurt.

In the end, the guy Tường decides to take a shovel from the porch and laboriously dig up the cave. When knowing for sure that Little Boy has truly disappeared, he lets go of the shovel and bursts into tears.

I enter the house just as my mom comes back home.

"What is all this digging and mess for?" My mom frowns and scolds Tường.

"My Little Boy . . ." Tường says these three words and then can't speak any more, just choking on sobs.

Little Plum has to support his words. "The toad, miss."

"How is it?" My mom asks, familiar with the toad.

"It's gone." Still it's Little Plum who answers. I can see her eyes getting red.

"Don't cry, dear! No need to cry! It's just off jumping around somewhere and will be back I'm sure."

My mom tries consoling Tường with an all-knowing voice, the way I've seen Mr. Xung calm down his patients while packing medicine for them: "Don't worry, Auntie Tám. Your sickness is very minor, just finish the medicine and you'll be back to health soon."

I don't know if Tường trusts what my mom says, but his tears gradually subside until all crying sounds are extinguished. He wipes his eyes, slowly stands up, and with Little Plum moves the bed back to where it was.

I clumsily try to lend a hand, for if I don't do at least this, I know my tangled heart will be tormented all night long. "Let me help you!"

52.
in which I'm regretful

My mom just says so, but I know for certain that Little Boy is never coming back home. It was lying in Old Mr. Five Bottles' pot and then it ended up in Melon's belly. It will never come back to my little brother again.

Tường doesn't know the extent of the situation as I do, but after three days he gets the feeling that he will not have the chance to meet Little Boy again.

From that time, Tường goes around totally dejected. No longer the happy-go-lucky kid he was every day before, he has even stopped sharing whispers with Little Plum.

Many times I run into him sitting and crying by himself in the back yard, with the fly swatter before his face and Little Plum sadly sitting at a distance from him.

Around this time, the First Mr. Hớn moves into Little Plum's house. After his own house collapsed, he rebuilt it and then sold that newly built house to Mr. Bé, the neighbor, so now Mr. Bé can knock down that house and use the land to farm.

Able to sell the house, the First Mr. Hớn earned enough, with the help of some loans, to buy Little Plum's house. Since the news of Little Plum's dad still being alive became known (as the burnt bones in the attic were not human bones), Little Plum's house is now worth more. Because the house sits right beside the main road, it's convenient for business.

I glance at Little Plum. I'm not sure if she's sad because her childhood home is now in the hands of someone else, or if she's sad because Tường is sad.

I approach Tường and hesitate before sitting down beside him. I mean to console him but when I start to open my mouth, I stammer. I feel that whatever sentence I will speak at this moment is more or less a lie.

To be honest, I didn't think my little brother would be so torn and adrift. I can say now, without fear of the sky falling on my head, that my regret is bottomless when seeing the pained look that has set in on Tường's face. I will curse myself for days.

Tường doesn't say anything either, though he knows I'm there sitting beside him. With his head hanging down, chin tucked into his chest, if a swooping sky were added onto his shoulders he'd look just like the painting of the punished Atlas that I've seen in the tales he often reads.

The two of us sit motionless beside each other for a long time. Finally, my lip quivering, I say, "Don't be sad, little brother! Just a few more days and Little Boy will be back home!"

I realize I have just called Tường "little brother" completely by accident, my voice noticeably softer.

"He's not ever coming back, Brother." Tường shifts his shoulders and hips, his gaze still fixed on the fly swatter before his face.

"How do you know that?"

"I just met with Melon. He was boasting that yesterday his dad caught a toad in our house."

Tường lets out a sob as he answers, his voice rising from some place suspended between his head and his chest, muffled. And though he's hunched over, I still see tears on his face.

"When no one was at home?" I feign innocence, my heart pounding. I summon a steel stomach just to not jump out of my chair.

"That has to be when. Because if mom, or you, or me, or Sister Plum had been home, there's no way Little Boy would've met danger."

I sigh a light breath of relief to hear Tường classify me among those who could have saved Little Boy from an uncertain fate. Surely Old Mr. Five Bottles just gave a general summary, not remembering my part in the story. I resolve in my gut to lock that secret inside me. Forever.

53.
in which the floods return

Before talking with Tường that day, I was thinking of combing the field's edge in search of another toad to surreptitiously leave under the bed. I would've said that finally Little Boy had come back, though I'm not sure Tường would've fallen for my ploy.

But now that idea has been extracted from my head. Tường knows Little Boy is no longer in this world, there's no pulling the wool over his eyes.

When I'm still contemplating how to redeem myself, a heavy rain suddenly claps down on the village. The rain sets into motion a series of events such that Tường no longer has the time nor the heart to bathe in his sadness over Little Boy, and for that I am eternally grateful.

At that time, low hanging black clouds were nearly touching the roof of the only church in town. The wind was heavy with humidity, a sign of the impending floods. In my village, the floods come in July and October. This year, though, just when the cicadas are starting to cry, the sky is already brimming with rain.

Last year and the year before, the flooding rains were similarly abnormal. My dad says it's because the climate of the earth is changing and because recently the forest upriver was relentlessly destroyed.

I fill the afternoons just sitting in my house and watching the clouds accumulate. Like soldiers gathering for roll call, the clouds converge every day in one thickness, slowly but dramatically, and when the sky is stretched tight with imminent water and reaches across the entire village, then the rains begin to fall.

Rain trickles down steadily from the morning until around noontime, at which point it's like the sky gets ripped open and rain bursts down. For the whole afternoon until evening, rain pummels in torrents against our thatched roof. The rain that leaks in makes it so no one in my house can get a wink of sleep. My mom, me, Tường, and Little Plum tear the house apart in search of anything that can catch the rainwater that continuously drops through the roof: a can, an aluminum tub, a plastic cup, a coconut shell, a bucket, a pot, a pan, a kettle, even our broken bowls.

It rains like a crazed beast: snarling, overwhelming, ceaseless. It feels like the black clouds have sucked the whole ocean up into the sky just so they can now triumphantly let it loose.

In the middle of the night, overflow from the mountain starts surging down. The water level slowly rises, nearly reaching the bed where my mom's worried gaze is fixed. Everyone in my house climbs up on the bed, each bringing a stool to sit on just above the water, and we huddle up to wait for morning.

Very fortunately, the flood only sweeps through our village one night. The next morning, the rains subside and water begins to gradually withdraw, leaving the road slick with mud, with countless pieces of trash, branches, animal carcasses that were caught in upturned tree roots, pieces of houses and fences. The post-flood scene is one of devastation, like the set of a war film that's wrapping up.

By lunch, it's time to itemize the damages: one of Mr. Four Cang's buffaloes floated away, one of Old Mr. Five Bottles' pigs died in the stable, Lady Thoan's kitchen has water damage, and Mr. Bé's new vegetable garden is now perfect for making a kids' soccer field.

But the biggest catastrophe is that the bridge crossing the Lồ Ồ Stream collapsed. Half the bridge remains with its structure just emerging out of the water, like the head of a person who's fallen into the stream and got their leg stuck, and the other half is surely downstream somewhere.

54.
an interrogation

Those are just the property damages.

It's the human damage that shakes the whole village.

The boy Melon, Old Mr. Five Bottles' son, keeps repeating that he saw with his own eyes Sister Vinh get swept away in the flood. He says he went out to pee and from his back yard he saw Sister Vinh fall in, drown, and get pulled down by the strong current. He said he screamed for help but no one heard him in the roaring wind. He went to go call his dad, but he only turned his head for a second and Sister Vinh was already washed far, far away, now just a tiny dot at the end of the paddy.

No one really knows if the boy Melon is making up the story or not, but it's true that Sister Vinh went missing after the flood. From noon to nighttime, the wailing cries have not ceased echoing from Sister Vinh's house.

Teacher Longan goes over to Old Mr. Five Bottles' house to get more information from the boy Melon. Everyone, adults and kids alike, circles around them like a swarming beehive.

Little Plum, the guy Tường, and I all eagerly contribute

to the pack of heads jamming together to hear Melon's story, a story that everyone's memorized already.

Old Mr. Five Bottles sits with his legs crossed, a posture that affirms he knows he's suddenly become an important figure. Scanning the crowd once then turning to the boy Melon who's standing with his arms obediently crossed before him, he slaps down on the table—*bang bang!*—startling the bunch of us kids, then speaks in a solemn voice.

"Remember, give full respect for whatever the teacher asks!"

"Yes, dear Father."

"Tell only what's true. Don't exaggerate or soften the details, remember?"

The boy Melon says yes again, his face white as paper. Perhaps he never expected that he could commit a crime just because he happened to see Sister Vinh get swept away.

All murmurs cease when Teacher Longan starts the interrogation.

"What time did you see Sister Vinh, little boy?"

"Dear Teacher, there's no clock in my house, so I don't know."

"Was it in the morning or afternoon?"

"Dear Teacher, it was in the morning. I often go pee in my back yard in the early morning."

Melon's candid answer creates a contagious giggle throughout the circle of kids. As the "hee hee" laughter spreads, the interrogation loses all traces of solemnity.

Teacher Longan hardens his face, hoping the severity of his appearance will restore order. But for us kids, even with hands over mouths, streams of squeaky mouse laughter leak out from between our fingers.

Old Mr. Five Bottles, after establishing his authority by thundering at his son, now simply takes a pack of rolling tobacco from his T-shirt pocket and idly rolls a cigarette, as if not involved at all.

Mr. Longan asks a few more questions yet finds nothing abnormal in Melon's answers. His face pales and his back droops, as if he's suddenly shrunk in size.

With a heavy heart, I take Tường and Little Plum's hands and lead them out from the crowd. "Ok, home, then!"

Tường's eyes are red. "So Sister Vinh is really dead, Brother?"

"How could she be dead! Who knows, someone probably saved her after she floated away!"

I know I'm being overly certain with Tường, but I feel my nose start to itch so I have to turn my face away.

At that moment, I see Uncle Dan.

55.

a merry tune

Uncle Dan stands among the crowd around Old Mr. Five Bottles' house. He's near the very back of the pack (perhaps afraid of being caught by Teacher Longan), which is why I didn't see him before.

As if sensing my eyes on him, Uncle Dan suddenly turns in my direction and when he sees me about to run over, he throws his hands up and gestures that I should go home first.

That evening, Uncle Dan comes over to our house.

I search his face for sadness, the kind of sadness that people wear during funerals, but he looks by no means sentimental.

He sits on the ground by the well, looking up to admire the dim figure of the moon hiding in a blanket of mist, and takes out his harmonica from his breast pocket to play.

His tune this evening is completely unlike that aching tune some days before.

I'm surprised to hear him play a marching song with an upbeat tone.

"What are you playing this song for?"

Uncle Dan puts the harmonica back in his pocket and says with cheer, "I'm going to go find Vinh soon."

Tường grabs Uncle Dan's hands, brightening up. "So you mean Sister Vinh is alive still, Uncle?"

"I guess so." Uncle Dan puts his arm around Tường's shoulder. "Miss Vinh has a kind face of good fortune, I'm sure someone will save her."

Little Plum blurts out, "Thiều just said the same thing this afternoon, Uncle!"

Uncle Dan bends down and puts his head close to ours, lowering his voice. "This here will be a secret mission. You guys can't tell anyone about it, ok?"

The three of us all agree, without having any idea that Uncle Dan will be leaving home that same night, late.

When opening my eyes the next morning, even before emerging from under the covers, I hear the voice of my grandma talking to my mom, which means that she must have come over first thing.

"Do you know where Dan went?"

"I don't know, Mom. Last night he was over here, but he didn't tell me anything."

My grandma asks, "Are the kids up?"

The guy Tường pinches my skin. "Oh, crap. What are we gonna say when Grandma asks us, Brother?"

After briefly pondering, I respond, "Just tell Grandma the truth."

"But Uncle Dan told us not to tell anyone."

"But if we don't tell her, Grandma is gonna worry."

Afraid that the guy Tường will resist, I smack my lips. "I don't think Uncle Dan would want Grandma to worry."

My grandma's forehead relaxes when she hears Tường and I relate what Uncle Dan said.

But a moment later, her frown returns. "Oh, that boy! Being washed away in the flood, what life is there to search for!"

56.
in which Teacher Longan comes over

The next day it's Teacher Longan's turn to come over.

Hand gripping a rattan switch, he shouts from outside the gate, "Where's the guy Dan?"

My mom steps out, politely greeting him, "Dear Teacher."

Tường, Little Plum, and I follow through the kitchen door, hurrying each other out to the back yard and then hiding beside the chicken coop to secretly watch.

Of the three of us, Tường runs the fastest. He hasn't forgotten his confrontation with Teacher Longan.

I have a clear view of the fury on Teacher Longan's face through the slits in the wall. He asks my mom with a harsh voice, "Ma'am, do you know where the guy Dan led Vinh off to?"

My mom shows some confusion. "I heard that little Vinh got taken in the current, sir."

"The current my . . . "

Teacher Longan is so utterly enraged that he forgets he's a teacher and nearly curses. At the last moment, he remembers who he's speaking to and catches himself to recover the sentence. "The current my . . . oh my! The current sweeps Vinh away one day and the next day Dan is missing. What's going on?"

My mom keeps her calm. "Surely Dan must be downstream, in the lower lands, trying to see if anyone could save Vinh."

At that moment, I hate Teacher Longan with a passion. He's always on a rampage and even now when speaking with my mom he is aggressive and rude, barking at her like she's one of his students. If he had a mane, he'd look just like a lion.

My hatred for him only cools when he comes back the next day, this time the usual rattan switch nowhere in sight. His demeanor is also quite changed, as if he'd only been wearing someone else's face before.

Teacher Longan sits down in a chair opposite my mom, face wearied as if having aged a decade in a day.

He says tiredly, "Please just be honest with me. I am asking you in sincerity."

"I already told you yesterday, Teacher."

Teacher Longan uses both hands to massage his temples, the gesture of someone with an agonizing headache. "The truth is I don't believe that Dan went to find Vinh. I also don't believe that Vinh was washed away in the current."

"What would give you the idea that—"

"I have the premonition of a father," Teacher Longan interrupts. "My daughter is still alive. I think that Dan and Vinh have drawn up some arrangement to go into hiding."

Tường, Little Plum, and I are crouched together eavesdropping outside in the yard, and when we hear that sentence, it's impossible for our faces not to impart astonishment to each other's eyes.

As if missing the bewildered expression on my mom's face, Teacher Longan raises his voice again, but this time it sounds as if he's begging. It's a voice I could never imagine coming out of lips that are so used to shrieking. A strange feeling.

"If you know where they are, please help me, I will be eternally grateful. Tell them that I will consent to the two of them . . ."

Teacher Longan's voice is suddenly overcome with a shadow, like it's being covered behind a handkerchief, and teardrops are creeping out from his crinkled eyes. My mouth drops, unexpectedly face to face now with a terribly difficult mood.

57.
the boy Melon

What we hear that day is a spark ready to ignite a controversy.

The second that Teacher Longan leaves the house, Tường asks, "Do you believe that story he told, Brother?"

"What story?"

"The story that Uncle Dan and Sister Vinh stole off into hiding somewhere outside the village."

Before I can give my reply, Little Plum is already answering, "I don't believe it. The boy Melon told me that he saw with his own eyes how Vinh got swept away in the current."

"What happens if the boy Melon was making it up?"

"Why would he make it up?"

Tường sticks all ten fingers into his hair and replies in bafflement, "How could I know that?"

He continues, gently glancing at Little Plum with the eyes of someone who's just learned they've made a mistake, "I just said 'what happens if.'"

Little Plum clicks her tongue and says, her voice becoming wise, "If the boy Melon was making it up, Teacher Longan would already know it. He pressed him with questions for several days until he no longer doubted the truth."

"Teacher Longan doesn't doubt it, but I doubt it." I shrug, feeling unable to stay silent anymore. "If Sister Vinh actually got swept away in the floods, then Uncle Dan wouldn't have been so perky like he was afterwards."

It seems that Little Plum's memory is awakened by my sentence. She quickly chimes in, abandoning the eloquent judgments she just gave, "Oh, yeah! I remember now, that day Uncle Dan didn't even show the tiniest bit of misery."

Tường spins his face to look at me. "So the boy Melon is making it up, then?"

"I can't say. Let's go find him and ask!"

Me and Tường come across the boy Melon by the banks of the Lồ Ồ Stream. He's squabbling with some little neighborhood kids over the position closest to the edge of the stream to be able to stand there and watch people building roads.

While the bridge is being repaired, a path is needed to cross the stream and resolve the highway's traffic. Buses approach the stream from one side and different buses depart from the other side. The guests have to get off with their luggage on one side and bring their things along a temporary dirt road, shuffling over to the other side by foot, then climb back up to another bus and continue their trip. It's called a "bus exchange."

The dirt road is nearly finished now, with adults and children alike standing on the banks to watch as if watching a concert.

I come up behind the boy Melon and tap his shoulder. "Hey."

Melon turns around and, seeing me, proceeds to growl, "I was here first, you can't make me leave!"

I purse my lips. "I'm not trying to take your spot."

I pull on his shirt. "Come over here, I got something important to talk to you about."

"What's so important?" His eyes are darting all over the place, looking alert.

"So come over here!"

After wavering and dilly-dallying, Melon follows me out to a spot in the rice field where Tường is sitting and waiting. As soon as he sees Tường, Melon immediately stops and asks in a worried voice, "The two of you plotting something?"

"Calm down!" I assure him. "I asked my brother to wait here to be my witness."

"Witness?" Melon widens his eyes, still not understanding what I want to say.

I kick my foot against a field divider, with a slight smile. "See here, my little brother is the "bluebird" of Sister Vinh and my Uncle Dan."

"Bluebird?" The boy Melon goes cross-eyed, looking at me as if I'm speaking Arabic.

"A 'bluebird' is a special messenger person." I have a big grin now while explaining. "Once upon a time my Uncle Dan and Sister Vinh sent letters to each other, entirely by the hands of Tường here."

When hearing this, Melon begins to get a sense of what's going on, seeming to guess the reason for my concern.

His face erupts in distress. "But what does that have to do with me?"

"What it has to do with you is up to you to understand." I snort for effect. "I just want you to know that whatever secrets my Uncle Dan has, he tells Tường here and so Tường knows everything."

The boy Melon avoids my gaze. He looks up to the sky. "Oh, yeah!"

This time I don't aim at the field divider. I kick my foot against Melon's leg. "'Oh yeah!' what?! You testify the truth now! Why did you make up the story that Miss Vinh drowned?"

Melon falls for my pretending to know, his face pales. "I'm telling you, you guys can't tell anyone about this!"

I'm beside myself with joy but my face maintains its composed scowl. "This story has to do with my uncle, how stupid a nephew would I be to tell it?"

This uncle-nephew relationship intimidates Melon so much that he loses his mind. He forgets that if my Uncle Dan's secrets are all safe with Tường, then the two of us wouldn't need to bother questioning him about anything.

That afternoon Melon spills nearly every secret he's got, basically turning his pockets inside out and shaking them vigorously. Me and Tường quickly pick up the secrets splashing out of him and put together this shocking story: Sister Vinh gave Melon money to make up the story that she drowned. She played some role of scriptwriter-turned-director, where Melon was the performer who would only repeat the lines she fed him. And so the whole village is fooled and Teacher Longan is spun like a merry-go-round around Melon, unable to discover a weak spot in his story!

At this point my heart is light as a feather. I look at Melon and ask through laughter, "So how much money did Miss Vinh give you?"

"I am helping Sister Vinh not for the money." Melon turns his face away. "Sister Vinh loves me the most. I also love her the most."

"Who told you that?" I put my hand on my chest. "Sister Vinh loves me the most. You are only loved the second best!"

Melon's mouth drops open to defend himself, and I see his jaw tighten, but then he doesn't say anything, only silently runs back to the stream's bank. Surely he remembered that I am the nephew of Uncle Dan. Sister Vinh loves Uncle Dan, so of course she loves his nephew the most.

58.

starving days

After the flood comes the famine for our village.

My village is a poor one. My dad couldn't find a job so he has to leave home to earn a living far away. In the city, his work is also unstable. All kinds of seasonal things, up and down, the salary is only enough for my dad to live on day to day, hand to mouth, while waiting for a better opportunity.

With news of the flood, my dad takes several days off to come back home and mend the thatched roof, rebuild the floor, and repair the bamboo fence. When the work is finished, he's immediately on his way out the door again, not concerned with making rhyming parodies for kids to sing anymore, and no longer wandering about from house to house telling stories of the Chinese heroes of swordplay, Xue Ding Shan and Fan Li Hua.

The famine becomes more and more apparent in the daily meals. Less rice in the pot. Fewer dishes on the tray. Fish and meat are sparse, and sometimes totally absent. Sometimes there are fried shrimp, but they're always terribly salty: shrimp coated in salt white as snow. I could eat three bowls of rice with just one of these "snow-shrimp."

Of course Tường, Little Plum, and I don't gripe and moan, but just looking at our waning faces, perhaps my mom can hear a sigh running throughout the meals, which clamps down on her heart.

For this reason, my mom agrees without even a moment's consideration when Mr. Four Cang invites her to join the wholesale buying trips so she can come back and sell things in the village.

In these hard days, if they have enough resources, some people build tents at either side of the bridge and sell soft drinks, eggs, bread, small pyramidal glutinous rice cakes, sesame candy, and peanut candy for passersby and bus-guests. If they don't have enough resources, people will spread a nylon mat by the roadside and carry the goods under their armpits to roam along the rows of buses parked next to each other.

One time, when going to pick the bamboo shoots across the stream, the guy Tường finds a piece of gold metal. He immediately runs up to show me and Little Plum.

"I found this, Brother!"

I take the piece of metal, inspect it carefully, then roar, "This is gold! Gold! Hey!"

Tường's eyes glisten. "Is it for real gold, Brother?"

"For real." I nod my head, beaming. "I once saw gold. The guy Sơn stole his father's gold and showed it to me. This is surely gold!"

Tường's eyes glisten even more as they widen. "This piece of gold'll be worth a lot of money, Brother?"

"Yes, a lot! A super, super lot!"

"One million dong?" Tường ventures a guess. In his mind, one million Vietnamese dong is a huge amount of money. But I'm the same. I've never seen a million with my eyes, only on the back of a lottery ticket.

"Yeah, a million." I whistle, adding, "Maybe even more!"

"Ten million, Brother?"

"Yeah, ten million!"

Tường claps his hands and screams, as if he's just pocketed the actual money.

"It's amazing! Our family's not poor anymore!"

I'm just as ecstatic as him. "From now on our family will be so rich! Richer than Old Mr. Huấn's family. I'll ask dad to build a three-story house, higher than the guy Sơn's!"

"And buy a car, Brother? The guy Sơn's family doesn't have any car," Tường eagerly adds.

I am generous. "Yes, of course. We'll buy a car."

Although I don't yet know how it feels to be the son of a rich family, just imagining how everything in my house will be better than the guy Sơn's, I feel a happiness rising in my body, something indescribable.

Tường puts a hand on Little Plum's shoulder. "And we'll share the money with Sister Plum too, Brother? So Sister Plum's house will be as rich as ours!"

Ah, I had totally forgotten. Tường's suggestion is truly obvious. I should have nodded my head and emphatically responded yes at that very second. But my inspiration is cut short when my eyes catch Tường's hand resting on Little Plum's shoulder.

As if a sharp knife has pierced the dreamy balloon in my heart, the joy of being rich immediately deflates. I let my eyes drop to my toes and clumsily utter, "Yeah."

Little Plum interprets my attitude in her own way, and her voice grows unbelievably sad. "I don't need it, friend. My mom just sold the house, so we've got money now."

"That's dumb!" My eyes flash up and I become senselessly angry. "There can't be much money in selling your house. This piece of gold is more than enough to buy ten houses like yours."

The guy Tường anxiously asks, "So, we will still share the money with Sister Plum, right, Brother?"

I get mad at Tường also, though he's moved his hand from Little Plum's shoulder. "Another dumb thing! If not sharing with her then who'd we share with?"

59.
the gold

As it sometimes happens, the day sprouts a long tail and seems to drag on through an endless afternoon, as if the sun were standing still.

From time to time, the guy Tường sprints to the middle of the yard, measures his own shadow, and then comes back in with the updated information: "My shadow's one part longer now. Mom'll be home soon."

For my part, I'm running out every few minutes to the main road, hopeful with every passing truck. Yet still no trace of Mom.

Mr. Four Cang trades cinnamon, sourcing it from an acquaintance who also trades this spice. My mom doesn't have much money, so she trades firewood.

The truck leaves early in the morning and comes back late in the afternoon, bringing different traders around to gather supplies to sell back in our village.

My mom's stop is the timber yards in a distant village. From there, she carries back home several logs cut by the cubic meter. My mom, Tường, and Little Plum then laboriously cut the wood into smaller pieces, while I am tasked with bundling them up for sale.

With Mom going out for trading supplies now, our meals are starting to have more meat. Every so often, she brings home a chicken, perhaps spending all her profits on it. To do business like this barely brings any profit, just compensation for your labor. But perhaps this is all my mom wants. Just to see our hungry eyes light up at the sight of a chicken dish in the middle of the tray. This is her happiness in those hard days.

But today we are not waiting on my mom to hear the squawk of a chicken in her hands like other days.

Tường and I take turns checking for her because we're itching to show her Tường's hot discovery. The thin piece of gold sparkles with magic in my imagination, like the magic wand of fairies in Tường's stories. Whoever's life is touched by the wand instantly transforms. My dad will no longer hopelessly roam the city and my mom will no longer have to toil from dawn till dusk.

I run out to the main road thirty-something times before the familiar truck stops at my gate and my mom steps down, a chicken cage in her hand. Mr. Four Cang and the driver help her roll the logs off the truck.

My mom sees me, now accompanied by the excited Tường and Little Plum after shouting into the house, "Hey Tường, hey Plum, Mom's home!"

"What are you guys waiting here for?" my mom asks with a voice that seems like scolding but with eyes that reveal her fondness.

"Mom, we're going to be rich!" The guy Tường joyfully bursts out before I have time to answer, showing her the piece of metal and dancing it over his head.

The truck noisily starts its engine and pulls away, covering up the sound of Tường's scream, so my mom can't clearly hear this big news.

Only when she's in our yard does my mom understand why the three of us have been so anxiously waiting and happy to see her. I proudly repeat Tường's previous declaration, "We're going to be rich, Mom!"

Though I think my mom can clearly hear it this time, she's not prepared to receive such sudden good news and gets confused. Perhaps she assumes there is some mistake in my words or her hearing.

"What's that, dear?" Mom looks at me, her eyes squinting in the sun.

I say with a glowing face, "Tường picked up a piece of gold over by the stream today!"

"See, Mom!" Tường gleefully places it in her hand. "We're going to be richer than Old Man Huấn!"

Mom takes the piece of metal and examines it closely while we anxiously observe her observing.

"We're going to share the money with Sister Plum, too!" The guy Tường remembers, and it's the fact that he never forgets Little Plum that riles me.

"Yes." My mom gives the metal back to Tường and smiles. "But this is bronze, not gold, baby. No one would buy this!"

Perhaps I will never forget this moment: my (and also the guy Tường's and Little Plum's) dreams blown apart. As if we were just about to touch Heaven's gate and the gate suddenly shut in our faces.

The three of us lifelessly turn our eyes to face each other. As if looking at the mirror, we each catch the sorrow and embarrassment in the other's face, and the bad mood lingers for many days.

60.
the cinnamon stick

I go over to Little Beg's house just once in those gloomy days.

Without enough to eat, we kids are too lazy to run and dance around as before, so the courtyards around Little Beg's house are mostly quiet.

I drop in on Little Beg's house not just for capture the flag or to play with leeches and turtles as usual; I want to give her a piece of a cinnamon stick.

To my friends and I, sticking a bit of fragrant cinnamon under our tongues and letting the taste spread around our mouths is an absolute delight, a rare pleasure. Whenever someone gives me a piece of cinnamon, I only dare to bite off a tiny piece, and I keep it in my mouth as long as possible, just breathing with it. Because the taste of cinnamon is a bit spicy, a bit acrid, a bit sweet, it's a kind of breath freshener.

After Mr. Four Cang gives me a piece of his cinnamon, I put it in my pocket and decide to save it for Little Plum. But with an intense craving, I cannot resist pulling it out and nibbling off a teeny piece from time to time. I only bite around the edges, around in a circle, until the cinamon piece is round as a coin. I decide I should run to find Little Plum.

I come into the back yard and see her and Tường shoulder to shoulder, with their heads inside some book, completely engrossed. The image boils my blood. The piece of cinnamon in my hand, I stick back into my pocket.

I no longer feel like giving Little Plum anything.

I resentfully make my way over to Little Beg's house that afternoon.

When I arrive, Little Beg is with some other kids playing follow-the-leader. I jog over to catch up with them and deliberately stand right behind her.

After roving around her yard for a while, I try to get her attention. "Hey, Little Beg."

"What's up, Thiều?"

Without even turning her head around for a second, she still knows it's me. Girls are crazy!

"I want to give you something."

"What is it?"

"Put your hand behind your back and find out!"

Little Beg puts her hand behind her back and I gingerly place the piece of cinnamon into her palm. I've given Little

Beg a letter before. But that time, I didn't dare go so far as to hand it to her myself, as the guy Sơn was my messenger. So I hadn't known about this mingling of nervous delight that happens when placing something into the hand of a girl who will then know how I like her.

I hold my breath as I watch Little Beg carefully take the piece of cinnamon in with her hands and eyes. My whole body rejoices when she brings the present up to her nose and exclaims, "Oh, cinnamon! Thiều, where'd you get this?"

"Mr. Four Cang gave it to me but I didn't eat it, I saved some to give you." I am overjoyed with my work.

Stifling your own desire and gifting someone else a piece of cinnamon—in my group of friends this is no less meaningful than handing down an inheritance. While I figure Little Beg will be incredibly touched and grateful, what she does is something I could never have predicted in my wildest imagination. She whips around to face my astonished face and sets the cinnamon back into my hand, saying in a frigid voice, "I won't take it! Go on and give it to your friend Plum!"

61.
the chicken meat

I am sunk for a few days after that.

So Little Beg knows I like Little Plum. But how could she know it when not even I am talented enough to guess it myself? But perhaps she saw Little Plum at my house, or she heard the guy Sơn spreading (and inventing) stories about me sleeping over at Little Plum's house the day her house caught fire. My weepy musings whirl around and around: why does life have to be so sad?

Little Plum still hasn't recognized my nervous and resentful attitude, though I am forced to witness her bent over playing with Tường all day.

And to make matters worse, my mom's business has been dwindling. The meals with chicken gradually taper off and I miserably return to those hungry days of being a little kid in a poor family.

Tường, Little Plum, and I just keep munching on sweet potatoes while my mom watches with concern.

One day when coming back from my grandma's house, I enter our yard and decide to take a stroll around the veranda to see what Tường and Little Plum are up to out there. But after a quick scan, I'm surprised not to see them anywhere.

When making my way to the kitchen, I suddenly detect the sounds of a whispered conversation coming from inside the house. I tiptoe up and put my curious ear to the wall to eavesdrop.

Of course it's Tường and Little Plum.

Tường says, "This piece of chicken is for you, here."

"And this is your piece here," Little Plum joyfully jumps in.

After some hardly audible sound on the table, I hear chomping and chewing.

My chest tightens. Tường and Little Plum are not only coupling off day after day, but they're also partnering with each other to sneak chicken behind my back. They must've done it many times, eating secretly like this when I'm not home. Just imagining it piques an anger in me with many targets, including my mom. Perhaps because there's less chicken meat to go around our house now, my mom has been sneaking it to just the two of them and neglecting me.

Mad, yearning, hurt: these dreadful feelings knit a tight fabric inside me and it's like I can't breathe. My body trembles uncontrollably so that I have to inch away from the wall to avoid making noise.

Echoes of their gushing meal invitations to each other play back through my mind and increasingly aggravate me.

"Go on, Sister Plum, and eat one more piece. The thigh here, I saved it for you."

"Thanks, Tường. Let me pick out a piece of the intestines for you."

I feel as if my whole body were on fire. I can't hold it in any longer—I burst into the house like a cow gone mad.

Completely out of my mind, when spotting Tường and Little Plum side by side at the table, I grab the dog-beating stick that my dad still keeps and batter it excessively against Tường's back. With each blow I snarl, "Chicken, eh!? Hiding from me, eh!? Eating in secret, eh!?"

Tường doesn't have a chance to answer. While suffering my blows, he can only cry out "Brother!" before falling to the ground.

My anger still not subsiding, I shoot an angry stare at Little Plum and see her with her mouth agape watching me, her eyes big as saucers. A look impossible to mistake: shocked, aghast, agonized. A look that will always come back to haunt me.

I haven't discovered my mistake by that point. When my eyes then fall from Little Plum's eyes down to the surface of the table I am dumbstruck.

Not one tiny piece of chicken anywhere.

The tabletop contains just some pieces of broken bowls that hold a few bamboo shoots, some pulled-apart ferns, and some small hibiscus leaves. What I see is the game of make-believe that kids in my village often play and one that I, not too long ago, also liked to play.

"Please, have some of this food!"

"Please, have some of the sticky rice with fish here! The fish was just caught from the river, so fresh!"

"Pass me the shrimp noodles, please! Remember to put in lots of shrimp!"

"Aren't these eggs delicious?"

Us kids would pretend to buy and sell food then invite each other to eat it. After that we'd pretend to chew loudly and hastily swallow, then nod in satisfaction. "So delicious!" "Delicious, just delicious!" Using the imagination would help to offset the difficulty of those years when food was scarce, help to satisfy cravings that were almost always smoldering in our hearts. A beloved game of kids in my village.

Those make-believe inviting sentences plus the innocent and pitiful dialogues, ones I had been accustomed to hearing every day, rise in my brain and start to bounce around my head, throbbing and biting and stabbing.

My regret feels like a sharp stake entering my head and plunging down to the bottom of my heels, securing me to the floor in wooden confusion.

My body is in shock and I don't realize that Tường is still lying on his back on the floor, languishing for some length of time, not waking up.

62.

in which something is not meant to happen

Little Plum rushes over to help Tường up, but she struggles for a while and still cannot budge him.

I only snap out of it when hearing Tường moan, "Brother, help me!" It shatters my heart to see him, a small animal shot to the ground by me, while I am also the one this poor wounded animal trusts to ask for help.

But when I hold his shoulder and try to lift him up by his armpit, Tường is just moaning, "Oh, it hurts!" I see his tears streaming.

I ask while quivering, "Where do you feel the most hurt?"

"In my back."

"Let me take a look."

I brush my hand over his back and press a finger on his spine to check.

Tường's face scrunches up. "It hurts, Brother!"

My forehead sweats. My father's beat us with this cane who knows how many times, but nothing this bad has ever happened.

Tường asks with grave worry in his voice, "Is something wrong with my spine, Brother?"

"Don't jump to assumptions!" I assure him and feel my nose start to get that hot tickle.

I turn my head and say through tightly pursed lips, "Just lie right here then, let me find a way to carry you to the bed."

But I can't figure out how. Tường's body now just exists as waves of pain, moaning with every touch. Moving him an inch seems as impossible as moving him up to the sky.

In the midst of my chaotic feeling, Little Plum's eyes light up and she yells while rising, "I got a way!"

"How?" I swallow, my mouth dry.

"Bring the wooden slats over here!"

Almost immediately, Little Plum and I shoot through the air to the bed where Tường and I sleep. We throw off the blanket and mat and hastily pull out the wooden slats at the bottom of the bed. We carry them to Tường and lie them down parallel to him.

"Just a bit longer. Try to endure, dear!" Little Plum gently reassures him while she holds on to his feet and I hold on to his head. We then cautiously move Tường, bit by bit, to put him on the thin wooden slats.

Tường bites his lips to not let the moaning escape, but just watching his writhing face, I know he's badly hurt.

Little Plum and I dare not make any sudden movements, which is why, for half an hour, all we can manage to do is shift the guy Tường up onto the wooden slats. It takes us another fifteen minutes to carry the wooden slats back to the bed, and carefully put him down.

63.
Mr. Xung

Because the truck doesn't come back until late afternoon, we can't just sit and wait for Mom. I wouldn't even know where to go in search of her anyway.

I tell Little Plum, "You stay here and look after Tường. I'm gonna run to find Mr. Xung."

"Go over to Grandma's house too and let her know too!" she reminds me.

"No." I wave my hand away. "If Grandma knew, she'd just worry her head off. Let's have Mr. Xung examine him first to see!"

As I'm about to go, Tường calls me back. His voice rises faintly from the mountain of blankets and pillows that we put around his body.

"Brother!"

I turn back, my heart softening when I hear his weak call. "What do you need, little brother?"

"Don't tell Mr. Xung that you beat me, Brother!"

Tường drills precisely into my anxiety. Since realizing I beat him in such a serious place, my stomach has been churning. I don't know what my parents will do if they find out I am responsible. My dad's temper is hot as fire. I'm sure he'll hang me by the neck, or at the very least kick me out of the house. And my mom. Perhaps Mom won't punish me, but I know her heart will be shattered, which is even more painful to me.

"If I don't tell him that, what should I say?" I look hard into Tường's eyes.

"Just say I climbed up the tree and fell to the ground, Brother."

As if someone has just removed a mountain from my shoulders, my heart is relieved. I turn to Little Plum and nervously wait for her response. She's the witness here, and if she doesn't agree, all bets are off.

Meeting my expectant and worried eyes, Little Plum's lips waver as she says, "Yeah, I think Thiều should cover up the story."

Tường carefully advises me, "And to our parents and anyone else, you also should say that I fell from the tree then, Brother."

I can't speak a word, just nod my head and quietly slip out of the house. I am a prisoner who's just been released without spending a day in prison (a release I was desperately hoping for). Yet when freed from the suffering, to my surprise my heart does not feel free at all.

The way Tường tries to protect me, even when he's the hurt victim, brings me horrible shame and torment. My dear little brother's love for me is so immense, despite how badly I always treat him.

On the way to Mr. Xung's house with such thoughts, tears blur my vision.

I bring Mr. Xung back to our house. I tensely watch as he takes Tường's pulse, inspects his eyes, checks his tongue, and touches his back, while continuously asking my little brother numerous questions.

Little Plum and I hold our breath and watch him. Time vividly stands still; everything Mr. Xung does seems to drag out interminably, like in a slow-motion film.

Our two mouths finally let out a slight exhale when Mr. Xung concludes his checkup and turns back to me, nodding his head and saying, "I'm hopeful that your brother's spine won't be injured. He's just been shaken up . . ."

There's more that Mr. Xung says, but my ears are just buzzing. When hearing that my brother's spine is ok, my heart bursts and no more words can enter my ears.

64.
the days after

My mom comes home and almost loses it when she learns the story of Tường climbing the tree, falling, and now being paralyzed, unable to sit up.

She runs over to where Tường is lying down, not scolding or blaming him, only sitting down by his side, running her hand through his hair, and crying. The guy Tường needs to repeatedly console her.

"Mom, don't be sad. Mr. Xung already said I just have to lie still like this for a few days. Just have to take some medicine for a few months and I'll be better."

Despite Tường saying this, despite me already having reported Mr. Xung's diagnosis, my mom still grabs her hat and runs like the wind to Little Beg's house to hear it straight from the expert's mouth one more time.

In the city, my dad hears the news from people in the village and hurries home too.

Opposite my mom, my dad stands at the foot of the bed, an angry scowl appearing on his face when he sees Tường.

"You can't be immobilized just from this. How many times have I beaten you with the cane already?!"

He turns his screams upon me. "It was you who started this asinine climbing game, wasn't it?"

"No, it was not." I shudder, stepping slightly back.

My dad chucks his bag down on the floor, snarling, "Damnit, Son!"

In those dark times, I honestly wasn't as afraid of my mom's crying or my dad's screaming as much as I was of the look on Little Plum's face. She looked at me silently and deeply, as if not looking at me but through me, to see what kind of toxic things my heart of hearts held. Perhaps she'd never be able to understand why I suddenly went insane that day, never be able to forget that violent face I wore when bursting into the house and taking the cane to rail against my little brother's back. Surely that image still haunts her.

Once I discover that Little Plum often steals looks at me, I try to avoid her face, the same way a criminal tries to shun the judgment that is perpetually weighing on their mind.

I only escape Little Plum's look when her mom gets released and comes to pick her up to go back home.

Little Plum's mom tells my mom that she will take Little Plum to go in search of her dad. As soon as I hear that, I feel light and sad at the same time, wishing for her family to be reunited.

The day of parting ways, the three of us cry together. Little Plum smoothes Tường's hair, her gesture exactly like my mom's, and says through snuffles, "Listen here, little brother. I'm going now. I wish you a speedy recovery."

Tường is also whimpering. "I wish the road rises to meet you and that you quickly meet your dad."

It's strange, but when I see this scene there's not even a tiny ripple of jealousy like before, only a concerned and heavy heart.

Little Plum and I say goodbye right before the gate.

Even though in recent days she has been looking at me with a kind of blame, at this moment she seems to not remember any of that.

She takes my hand and holds it tightly, eyes welling up with tears.

"Stay strong and well, please, Thiều!"

This is the first time Little Plum is the one who takes my hand. That other time, beneath the mountain pepper tree when hearing how she usually suffered her mom's excessive beatings, I was the one who first took her hand. My heart is uneasy. I think I'm going to confess everything to Little Plum, but I inexplicably and suddenly forget almost my whole vocabulary.

With a dry mouth, I only manage, "Yes, you too, Plum."

This is the first time I address Little Plum by her name, but it's not even a little bit awkward, it's as if I've called her like this many times before.

"I'll come back to visit you one of these days, Thiều."

It is while following her mom out that Little Plum looks back at me with a pair of wet eyes and says this last sentence, which I know not even she is sure will happen.

She is still small.

65.

more days after

Since Little Plum's departure, life has become endlessly dreary.

The only thing that brings some joy is that Uncle Dan sent some news home. He said that he and Sister Vinh are living very far away and are very happy.

He wrote how he'd heard that Teacher Longan was ready to accept him and Vinh, but that he'd come home first by himself to check. If the teacher was sincere about him and Sister Vinh being together, then the couple would come back to the village to live and take care of their parents on both sides, which means my grandma and Teacher Longan.

While waiting for Uncle Dan to come back, I hover every day over Tường's bed. The bed used to be against the wall in the inner room, but now it's been moved beside the window, according to Tường's wishes. He can't go out, so he wants to lie down where he's able to admire the clouds and the sky, sometimes spotting a flock of birds flying past. Tường says it's what he wants, and there's no reason to not follow his wishes.

I spend nearly the whole day by his side, talking to him, entertaining him, helping him move to the bathroom.

Actually, for taking him to the bathroom, it's my mom who cares for that. Since the day Tường met this misfortune, my mom stopped selling firewood so she could stay home and nurse him. My mom is well aware of how I am the lazy child who always avoids unpleasant things.

And so, she is happily surprised to see me caring for Tường as diligently as possible, not minding anything at all, and even more, having an enjoyable attitude—qualities that she didn't think she'd ever see me have.

"I didn't know you loved your little brother so much!" Mom once praised me, with a voice full of emotion.

Of course I was not warmed by the praise of my mom. On the contrary, the feeling that flooded my body at that moment was shame. If my mom only knew that it was me who made Tường this way, she'd surely be so disappointed in me.

Luckily for me, when my mom utters her praise of me she and I are in the front of the house, so it cannot reach Tường's ears.

In those days, neighbors took turns visiting Tường and consoling my mom. Someone gave us banana bread, someone gifted us oranges, someone brought us a can of milk. Our village is a poor one, so the gifts are not really worth anything, but everyone's kindness is still enough to distract my mom from her worry.

The only exception is the guy Sơn. One morning his dad comes over to give my mom a dozen eggs; that evening I see Sơn standing outside looking in the window, a big grin on his face.

"What do you want?" I suspiciously ask when seeing him leaning halfway through the window.

"I'm trying to see if the guy Tường is dead yet." With his lip curled, Sơn's eyes incessantly roam around the place where Tường is lying.

"You ignorant ass!" I raise my fist up to his face, feeling the blood rush to my head.

Sơn shrugs his shoulders, his voice fully satisfied. "The other day it was him who was threatening to kill me. Who knew that the one who made threats would be the one to die first."

I shoot a wad of spit in his direction but do not hit him, and I growl, "Now you're gonna be the one who dies first!"

Sơn takes a step back to dodge the second wad of spit, and he says, his voice suddenly more gentle, "I actually came just to give a cure to your little brother."

He wipes his hand across his nose. "I know a way of curing this illness."

I hesitate before speaking, my eyes stuck to Sơn's face, wondering if a no-good kid like him could ever be kind. "My little brother is taking medicine from Mr. Xung."

"Oh, my! Such a cornball kind of medicine like that, what actual help can it be?" Sơn raises his two hands up to the sky, a sneer stretched across his face as if he were talking about some rotten cucumbers.

I half believe and half doubt him. "So you know another way to heal him, then?"

"Yeah."

I'm nearly holding my breath. "What's the way?"

Sơn's eyes light up, the jerk. "Rub chili powder in his eyes."

It's like he just landed a blow to my neck. I unleash a roar and I bend down to take a sandal from the floor, then I throw it out the window.

But Sơn's no longer there. The sound of his arrogant laughter gradually fades from over the gate.

"Leave it alone, Brother!" Tường puts his hand on my hand.

"How to leave it alone?!" The suppressed anger bursts out. "If he so much as steps foot near our house again, I will beat him into another life. I will be ready with the cane to—"

I suddenly bite my tongue.

I sigh, remembering that very cane is what laid my brother out like this.

66.
Little Plum's secret

I'd never thought of Little Plum as also having secrets. When I learn what she's been concealing in her heart during our past days together, my body suddenly stiffens.

That day, I take my dad's Chinese chess board over to Tường and place it on his chest so we can play tic-tac-toe. I prop the board up and stack more pillows beneath Tường's head, giving him some comfort to play.

We each have a piece of charcoal: I mark 'o', he marks 'x'. After just a few games I am already getting crushed. I don't understand how he can be so bad at studying but so excellent at tic-tac-toe.

Tired of losing, I toss my charcoal and move the board away. "I surrender. You're too good."

Tường smiles. "But when I play with Sister Plum, I'm always a loser."

When Tường brings up Little Plum, my face unconsciously collapses. I turn my eyes to take in the sunlight sparkling on the branches outside the window, pondering in quiet sadness which part of the sky she and her mom are meandering under now, and if they have met her dad. I don't know when we'll be able to meet again. That day we parted, the last thing Little Plum said was a kind of promise of return, but it tastes bitter now, so far away.

"Sister Plum likes you a lot, Brother!" Tường breaks the silence.

As if a bullet flew over my head, I startle, and whip around to face him. "What'd you say?"

Tường smiles and looks at me with his mischievous eyes. "Sister Plum told me that she really likes playing with you."

I blush. I have to twitch my mouth to convince myself

I'm not dreaming. Little Plum likes me? And she confided in the guy Tường? In a single second all these thoughts pile up in my mind. I recall when I told her she was the only one I liked to play with, and her response was that she also liked playing with me. But I thought that was something of the past already. The whole time Little Plum was staying with us, her attitude toward me was so distant. From morning to night, she was only attached at the hip to the guy Tường, enough to drive me crazy.

"If she likes me, why'd she just buddy up to you all the time?" I voice the wonder in my head, trying to stay composed and avoiding looking directly into Tường's eyes.

"Sister Plum is shy, Brother."

I exhale a long *phhhh*. "We've been close since we were little, why pretend—"

I stop myself halfway. Oh, how stupid I am! Being close since we were little kids, when it was only pure friendship was one thing, but now her feelings for me and my feelings for her are totally different. Exactly how the feelings are different, I'm not so sure, but I know nothing is like it was in the old days.

And not the least: Little Plum is a girl. She can't act as naturally as a boy can.

In the middle of these meandering thoughts, there's a sudden flicker in my brain, as if someone struck a match inside my head. That's it! Surely every detail was imprinted in her memory, the night she took her pillow and blanket to sleep next to me. It was the first night she had to sleep alone, after her house partially burned, and she feared the ghosts, the loneliness, the desertedness, everything. That night, the fear was so overflowing that it dissolved her shyness. But the next morning, recalling it, she must have been so embarrassed. That's it: after that night, she always found ways to avoid me.

Liking to play with me and yet not daring to play with me, Little Plum must have been so sad. But I was unfairly suspicious of her and of my little brother too! Hello, stupid!

67.
the dwelling of sadness

It's now been three weeks since Tường started taking Mr. Xung's medicine.

Mr. Xung keeps reassuring us that Tường will be fine, will soon be free of pain, that he just needs to finish the medicine and he'll be good to go. But I don't see any sign of improvement.

Tường can move a bit now, of course, and it's getting less painful, but he still can't sit up.

Seeing my mom's worried face, Tường says, "Mom, don't worry! I'll be able to sit up soon."

He tells me the same.

I get irritated. "'Soon' a monkey's ass!" I swear at him, but my eyes fill with tears. I feel sorry for him and sorry for myself. Watching him lying there stiff as a doornail, it feels like someone is trampling on my heart.

In such moments, Tường often steers the talk in another direction. "Let's get the chess board and play tic-tac-toe, Brother?"

Until now, he still hasn't spoken even one word about the fact that I beat him for no reason. I know he loves and cares for me so much, he doesn't want me to be tormented by guilt. But his sweet behavior somehow torments me even more.

I look at him pitifully. "Tường, ah, I'm really sorry . . ."

He takes my hands and speaks as a grown-up would. "It's not your fault, Brother. It's my fate, like the fortune-teller said. If you didn't happen to cause this injury, sooner or later I'd have actually fallen from the tree or gotten mixed up with Mr. Four Cang's mad buffalo. And I'd be just as much of a log as I am now!"

Somehow even this soothing compassion tastes bitter in my mouth.

I have to run away to hide the tears streaming down my face.

In those days, my fear of worms spontaneously vanishes. I can go dig in the garden and find some millipedes and hairy worms to bring in for Tường to play with, and some sticks.

I wander by myself in the heat of noon, sit in wait to catch cicadas, pick the seed bones from flamboyant flowers to play chicken with him. I can do everything for my little brother. The only thing I can't do is bring back Little Boy for him.

At this time, the new bridge over the Lồ Ô Stream is completed.

Rice is planted throughout the fields and the verdant green starts to rise toward the sun.

In Mr. Bé's garden, the vegetables are bountiful.

Children in the village, after days of roaming around the bridge to sell things, now gather back up in Little Beg's yard to play. Familiar laughter returns.

Sadness melts slowly, slowly away.

It stagnates only in one place.

My house.

68.

an abnormal occurrence

I start to drown in hopelessness about Mr. Xung's ineffective packets of medicine. I have a dreadful sense that the guy Tường will have to drag out the rest of his days on this earth like this, lying on his back in bed, only able to look at life from the perspective of below.

Summer floats by and I consider abandoning school for the year to come so I can stay home and nurse my little brother.

That idea, as soon as it's planted in my mind, takes root and I try to get used to the fact that even Sơn and Little Beg will look down on me from the next grade in school.

A future like that would surely be a rough one, but I know I can overcome the shame of my friends teasing me. That's why I don't consider it that much. The biggest obstacles will be persuading my mom and dad, which is something far less simple than climbing a ladder up to the sky.

My head in those days is like a saturated sponge of worry. And while I still haven't thought of how to begin talking to Mom and Dad so that the talk ends favorably for me, something abnormal occurs.

At lunchtime, I go to grind rice powder at Lady Thoan's house and when I come back home, I just step through the door and see something so shocking that I drop the bag, and its milky white contents spill out all over the floor.

Not wanting to clean it up, not scared of a lecture from Mom, I just keep standing there, eyes fixed on Tường, mouth agape as if a piece of apple got stuck in my throat.

I've never seen a ghost, despite being petrified of them, but if I ever did see a ghost, I think even that feeling wouldn't compare to this moment.

Before my eyes, the guy Tường is sitting straight up, for who knows how long already, looking vaguely somewhere outside the window. He doesn't see me enter the room.

Only when hearing the powder bucket crash to the floor and its handle make a loud clank does he turn around.

"Brother!" his voice rings out, his eyes radiant. "I can sit up now!"

With a great deal of effort, I struggle to find my voice. But I can only manage to stammer, "You . . . you . . ."

"Brother! I just saw a princess!" Tường is beaming with this news.

"A princess, eh?" I ask mechanically, still not understanding what he meant to say, though I believe I've heard him clearly.

"That's right, a princess." Tường nods and then sees my face frozen in disbelief. He stifles a laugh and adds, "Like in the *Fire-Bellied Toad* story."

Suddenly a sharp pain stings in my chest. I carefully inspect Tường's ecstatic face, trying to believe that it's not the face of someone showing signs of nerve damage.

"Oh, I remember . . . yeah, the *Fire-Bellied Toad* story . . ."

I mumble an indifferent answer, not wanting to say anything that would upset him by accident, while watching him and urgently sifting through some thoughts in my head.

I remember the *Fire-Bellied Toad* story, a story Tường particularly loves. I think it's no coincidence that he cherished that toad under the bed so much that his whole face was swollen with tears the day that Little Boy said goodbye to this lifetime.

I also remember the question he once asked me: "Are princesses real in this life, Brother?" The dreamy expression on his face when asking told me for sure that he was fanta-

157

sizing about the Princess in *The Fire-Bellied Toad*, and of course he himself as the Prince in that crappy story.

"Perhaps they were once upon a time, but not anymore," I had answered at that time, and I think my reply must have stuck because I never heard him repeat that foolish wondering again.

And so now he's talking gibberish like someone who's just banged their head against a tree.

Trying to contain the shaking in my leg, I keep a placid voice while continuing to probe. "Where did you see the Princess?"

"Just before, she was standing by the window. She lifted up her face to see me and just kept smiling at me, Brother," Tường answers in an exceptionally gleeful voice, clearly not yet recovered from his excited state.

I ask again, this time my voice beginning to crack, "So the Princess was standing outside the window, for real? You sure you're not a bit dizzy?"

"It's for real, Brother!" Tường opens his eyes widely, it seems with complete astonishment at my doubtful question. "When the Princess left, I rose to watch her go. And . . . I could sit up on my own, I didn't even know!"

"So it's all thanks to seeing the Princess off?" I ask in a way that may seem sarcastic but is completely sincere, just to express my amazement.

"Yes."

Tường nods his head and then without waiting for me to ask anything else, he expertly recounts, "The Princess is beautiful, Brother. She wears a dark green dress, with puffy sleeves and pink lacing. She keeps her hair in pink ribbons. On her neck she wears a string of purple jade too . . ."

I can tell from the look on my little brother's face that he is sinking into reverie. It's as if his face is disappearing

158

behind a curtain of mist, and he's still looking at the Princess with every word he speaks.

I asked him to describe the appearance of the Princess in order to check if his brain is malfunctioning or not, and the way he described her with so many details and such emotion, it's impossible for me not to believe that there was a princess standing outside the window smiling at him this morning.

69.
the Princess

Perhaps there's no ink that could note my mom's joy when seeing Tường sitting up in bed.

Without wasting a moment, my mom runs over to Mr. Xung's house to thank him profusely and invite him over.

Mr. Xung's face is all smiles, and he expresses his cheer by continuously clapping his hands. "I told you, already! I told you, already!"

Naturally, I don't mention anything to my mom about the strange Princess by the window. I also advise Tường not to spread the word about it to anyone else. When he gives me a quizzical look, I have to explain that she's a mystical secret only us brothers can know.

I'm only afraid my mom will freak out when hearing that implausible story. Surely my mom will think Tường's brain is not normal, just as I thought at first.

Of course, now I've seen Tường's story through other eyes. I suppose the Princess that he describes in such detail could actually be what he saw. If it was an illusion, Tường couldn't have so clearly remembered each detail of her dress like he did. And even the detail of her age.

As my mom is letting Mr. Xung out the door, Tường turns to me, perky and full of life. "The Princess was quite young, actually. About the same age as me, Brother!"

I almost ask, "Are you sure about that?" but I sense there's no point to that question, so I make up another one. "So, did the Princess say anything to you?"

"The Princess didn't say anything. She just raised her face to look at me. Then smiled. After that she went away."

I consider asking, "Which direction did she go in?" but once again I change my mind. If the Princess were real, then surely it'd be impossible for Tường to know where she came from and where she was going. I guess that she came from the cemetery, because the window beside Tường's bed faces in that direction. That inference doesn't sit so well, though. I try to banish the idea of a ghost from my mind, but the hairs on the back of my neck are already alert.

Two days later, the Princess appears again, right when my mom sends me over to Mr. Bé's house to buy baby cabbage.

When I come back home, the mysterious Princess has already left and Tường is standing up with his arms resting on the windowsill, looking outside.

I am not as taken aback this time, but the delight in my heart is like a balloon blown up to double the size it was when I first saw Tường sitting up in bed.

A scream peals out of me, "Oh! Tường is standing! Hey, Mom!"

That day is like a party. My mom's eyes well up with tears and she again goes out to find Mr. Xung.

The guy Tường can put his leg down on the ground, can stand up by himself, but cannot yet take a step. Even though he's able to stand steady, he still needs to hold on to the window. But anyway, it's a breakthrough event that my mom radiantly boasts about to the whole village.

I'm honestly not sure if the transformation in Tường's condition was caused by the medicine or the appearance of the Princess, or both. Of course the cause is nothing compared to the effect that came about, but I'm still curious and ask Tường when the two of us are alone, "So, does the Princess still come by?"

"Yes."

"Does she still wear that dark green dress like the other day?"

"Yes." Tường blinks his eyes and tosses his silky hair. "But today the Princess's ribbons are white."

I squint my eyes. "So this time did the Princess say anything to you?"

"Yes." Tường blushes. "The Princess just said . . . just two words, Brother."

"What two words?" I ask and gently take his hands into mine, as if trying to transfer some courage for him to speak, scared that he might not tell me anything at all.

Tường looks baffled. It seems hard work to bring the answer to his lips. In a barely audible voice, such that I have to bend my ear and watch his face closely to guess what he (and the Princess) said, he tells me, "The Princess said, 'My Prince.'"

I nearly guffaw, but catch myself before making that graceless gesture. I try to arrange my voice to be neutral but still cannot hide a little hint of ridicule. "So the Princess called you 'my Prince,' then?"

Tường looks elsewhere, seeming to sense the mockery in my voice.

"So the Princess chose you, then. You will be the Prince, with the status of chancellor. Like in the story."

I tease Tường but am considering it deeply. I'm convinced my brother has seen a girl he believes to be a princess.

161

It's impossible for a delusion to come back twice like that, and except for the story about the Princess by the window, all of Tường's behavior and words are normal. There are no warning signs that he was just bitten by a mad dog.

70.
where the Princess is from

From that day on, I resolve to not go anywhere, though my mom gets on my case for being lazy.

For both appearances of the mystical Princess, I wasn't home. So I decide to not go out for a whole week, in the hopes that I'll see with my own eyes what Tường saw.

I believe if there's really such a princess, surely she'll come visit her "Prince" Tường again.

Those days of waiting crawl by at a snail's pace. Every morning, I run across to the other side of the road and hide myself behind a peony bush. I just sit there with my eyes glued anxiously to the window of the room where Tường is lying. Sitting for a while without seeing anything, I trot back home to play with Tường, and then later find another reason to go out.

I put my sandals under my butt for a cushion and stretch my legs out on the grass to rest, observing the spot and meandering around in my thoughts. I wish that Uncle Dan were still here, so I could ask him about the Princess. Surely he'd tell me if the Princess was real or not, and why she came to our village. As well as the King and the Queen. Who are they? Where's their kingdom?

My thoughts then wander to Tường's Little Boy. The toad died already, but its spirit still somehow protects its owner. Though it doesn't possess the jewel of life-restoring powers like the fire-bellied toad in the fairy tale, perhaps it still returns night after night in secret and quietly transfers strength back into my little brother's legs. It brings along with it a mystical princess from a faraway place, which gives my little brother such an incredible joy that he forgets all about his miserable pain.

I sit and sit, think and think, and by the fourth day, I am bored. I also fear being seen by my friends in the village, who will wonder why I'm sitting here and I won't know how to answer.

On the fifth day, just as the thought of giving up crosses my mind, I see what I've been waiting for.

A princess, a beautiful princess, appears from somewhere in the middle of the cemetery, running like the wind in a pair of embroidered slippers. While moving toward my house, it seems she's floating above the grass; the sparkling lace down the arms of her dress and the string of jade around her neck glisten in the early morning sun. From a distance, it all looks like stars moving through the daylight.

My heart flutters and I soundlessly rise when seeing her sneak through the wobbly fence behind our garden and enter the yard.

My first impulse is to sprint as fast as possible back to my house, but after a second thought, I feel it's better to watch from afar.

I decide to hide myself behind the peonies, squinting to get a good look and with a swarm of questions fluttering in my head.

Exactly as I thought, she tiptoes up to the window and peers inside. I can't tell if she's smiling at Tường or not, or if she's saying anything, but her gestures appear quite cheerful. After a few moments, I see my little brother's head rise to the window.

It seems the two of them are exchanging words, very quickly, perhaps each just speaking one sentence, because right after that Tường disappears from the window frame. I assume that he sits back down on the bed because his legs are getting tired or sore, but it turns out I'm wrong.

Tường pops back up, this time at the door by the side of the house. I have to rub my eyes two or three times just to confirm that it's actually him, walking again. I could jump with joy and feel my heart dancing inside my chest.

Tường stands still in one place, bracing himself on the door frame. Perhaps he's not able to go any farther. While I thought the little Princess was going to step toward Tường, she simply lifts her hand to wave goodbye (perhaps with a smile) and turns toward the fence.

After that fleeting moment of being transfixed, I snap into action and try to chase after the Princess with all my might.

71.
where the Princess lives

The Princess leaves me in the dust.

I probably could've caught up to her, but Tường was still standing at the door watching her leave, so I couldn't follow directly behind her.

Instead I have to take the long way back behind Little Plum's old house to stay out of Tường's sight. By the time I finally reach the grass at the cemetery's edge, the Princess is just a distant speck.

It means she doesn't come from the cemetery. It means she's not a ghost. The thought relaxes me a little bit. But just as the color returns to my cheeks, another thought turns me pale again.

It dawns on me that what's on the other side of the cemetery—Withering Grass Hill and farther on, Black Cat Hamlet—is perhaps a thousand times scarier than the cemetery.

I've never set foot in Black Cat Hamlet. My parents don't have any acquaintances there, and actually, no one has the nerve to build a house there except for Mr. Tám Tàng, the former shaman-turned-pig-slaughterer.

The guy Sơn tried frightening me with that story about a tiger with an injured leg, who could hear human voices, who resided in the forest clearings of Black Cat Hamlet. At first I didn't believe his story at all. But after Uncle Dan gave his own statement about the place, I started to half doubt, half believe it. And then, after learning that all my friends were forbidden from wandering into that area, all doubt was erased.

Could it be that the Princess is the tiger ghost transfigured to tempt my little brother? The burning question smolders in my mind, and I bring my hands to my hair in a gesture meant to extinguish the fiery fear. Meanwhile, I keep walking.

To tell the truth, when seeing the strange princess ascend Withering Grass Hill without any sign of stopping, my legs want to turn back. But after a brief spell of wondering, curiosity takes control of my fearful legs and pushes them forward.

This is the first time I have climbed Withering Grass Hill. For so long, my friends and I would spend whole windy afternoons out on the huge grassy fields of the cemetery, playing and running around, flying kites, picking up dry cow dung and burning it to attract the stink bugs. But never before have I climbed up the hill.

Even without knowing the myth of Black Cat Hamlet, I felt feverish whenever directing my gaze toward the deserted Withering Grass Hill. The bare landscape with charred dry fields, the date palm bush's scattered greens—such images gave me a nameless melancholy.

Black Cat Hamlet is deserted in a different way. It has more green than Withering Grass Hill, which is bathed in the yellow of dry land and burnt grass.

But though wearing a different color, Black Cat Hamlet is still a bleak landscape with the spooky feeling of a ghost tiger lurking somewhere in its dark corners. The only bright point I can imagine is the Princess, walking among the sparse trees.

The Princess slows her pace now, and I see she is holding a bouquet of colorful wildflowers that she must've picked up sometime along the way.

As she merrily ambles through the field, picking up more flowers, catching butterflies, I have the chance to close the distance between us. I have to constantly remind myself to be cautious and remain hidden.

I'm amazed to realize that my fear of ghosts has vanished. I totally forget about the ghost tiger, being so focused on the Princess this whole time and there being no sign of any cursed tigers spirits in this forest, unless the Princess herself is one. But my instincts tell me it's unbelievable.

Finally the Princess leaves the forest, or the forest gives up the Princess. To me it's the same, as the forest must run out of trees sooner or later.

A thatched roof, like that of many other houses in our village, appears before me as I follow the Princess out of the forest.

When she's just about to reach the gate, a scolding cry from within the house rises. It is an angry voice that does not conceal its tenderness, perhaps coming from the mouth of someone between two attitudes: "Where were you off to, my child?"

72.
the King and the Princess

The scream shocks me and I quickly slip into a tree trunk.

I am shocked once more when, after the scream, a man steps out from the house.

My mouth gapes open: a proper king.

The man wears a silver crown that clings to his head, his hair beneath it shooting out in all four directions like a wild mane. He wears a long, white shirt that reaches his heels. Wrapped around his chest is a scarf that seems to be made of fur. And even though there's no war or enemy to fight, in his hand there trembles a precious sword.

"Dear King, I was just going around the forest is all."

The Princess's reply causes my jaw to stiffen and it's impossible to open it further. Could it be that the Princess is real and that man there is a real king?

"My dear Highness." The King drops his sword. "This is not the first time you haven't obeyed me."

"I'm sorry, dear King," the Princess answers, though it seems she's neither apologetic nor afraid of anything, perhaps because she's assured of the King's immense love for her. She prances back into the house, it seems truly fresh and happy, like the flowers swinging in her hand.

The King watches as she goes, sighing, "Poor you, my dear child."

This time, the voice of the King seems incredibly familiar. When I remember that there's only one person who has dared to build house in Black Cat Hamlet, I realize in that moment who the King is: none other than Mr. Tám Tàng himself, the one who slaughters pigs.

As if I were knocked over the head, my brain temporarily

goes blank. When I come back to, the King—or no, now it is Mr. Tám Tàng—has disappeared behind the door.

Five minutes later, I find myself by the side of the house, nervously peering through the small gaps between the planks of the wall, just like when I'm squeezing beside my friends to steal a peek at the traveling carnival that sometimes passes through my village and performs in the empty field.

Inside, Mr. Tám Tàng sits in a chair, the crown still on his head but the sword now laid down on the table. When seeing him up close like this, his face seems quite creased, exhausted, no longer like a king. An aging actor.

The Princess occupies herself in the kitchen, occasionally answering the King's questions while continuing to lift up the lids of pots in search of something to eat.

The words "King" and "Highness" that are mixed inside their questions and answers are no longer shocking, just amusing.

"Dear King, I've seen a prince."

The Princess's sudden declaration is followed by a turn of her body to look into the King's eyes.

Outside by the wall, I am tightly biting my lip to avoid losing my mind.

"You've seen a prince?" Mr. Tám Tàng objectively repeats the information, the significance of which seemingly having not yet sunk in.

"Yes," the Princess answers in a radiant voice, as if now finding something she can eat in the cupboard. "A very handsome prince, dear King."

As if suddenly grasping what the girl said, the eyebrows of the King lower. "Oh, so it is *the* Prince!" His eyes swirl to meet her eyes with a tense look. "Where did you meet him?"

"Yes, over by the cemetery . . ."

I see Mr. Tám Tàng's jaw fix into place, an unmistakable

sign of anger. But when speaking with the Princess, he makes every effort to maintain a calm and restrained voice so as not to sound frightening. "My dear Highness! How many times have I said, 'You are not allowed to go over the top of the hill.'"

The Princess knows the King is not pleased. She drops her eyes and quietly stands there.

I look more closely at her and realize her shirt is old, surely made of a cheap fabric, and carelessly dyed, with its green faded in several spots.

And the necklace she wears is perhaps not jade, nor any kind of stone. It seems to be made from the kind of colorful plastic beads that people sell at the gate of our school.

"I've told you that over the hill is the enemy kingdom. If you accidentally meet anyone, they can kill you immediately."

My head is ringing. A feeling of sadness and pity takes hold of my body. Clearly, both Mr. Tám Tàng and his daughter are crazy. He's slaughtered so many pigs that surely the ghosts of the pigs have taken their revenge, haunting both father and daughter, turning his house into a cryptic theater. Try as I might, I cannot get the idea out of my head that they have been forced by fate into this other world, melancholy and vacant, secluded from the world of people—not only geographically.

Dazed in disbelief, I let one hand slip and it knocks into a hoe leaning against the wall, which topples over into a metal washtub beside it. *Crash!*

Aghast, I quickly cover my mouth, as though, if my fingers can conceal the scream then maybe I am just imagining that ringing and clattering that spurt out of my mouth.

In these moments, I want to convince myself that nobody in the house noticed, or if they did notice, then they didn't pay attention. But Mr. Tám Tàng has already sped over to the wall by the time I turn around. I am stunned to see him standing there by the door, just as he is stunned, once he puts on his glasses, to see me.

After the initial shock, of course, comes anger. He sputters and the twitching of his face muscles distorts his face.

"You . . . you . . ."

73.
the King's sword

I'm sure my face also deforms out of fear.

And I hear my own sputtering, as if I left my voice at the edge of the forest.

"Uncle . . .Uncle . . ."

I mean to say "Uncle, please let me go," though I'm not exactly sure what I'm guilty of, but my tongue has disappeared somewhere in the back of my throat.

It seems Mr. Tám Tàng has decided to do something—the sword in his hand trembles—but at that moment the Princess appears beside him. Just like the King's reaction, her sparkling black eyes widen with the shock of seeing me. She must be astonished, not having seen a human figure around this area for so long.

Mr. Tám Tàng's attitude immediately changes when the girl steps out.

All his anger disappears, with not even a trace of it lingering on his face, as if someone just washed all his fury away. By the time he starts his first full sentence, he's already composed his face with the serious look of a king.

"What is your business with His Majesty?"

I stand there dumbfounded for a bit. My speechlessness only partly dissolves when I glimpse him winking at me, and the rest totally dissolves when I can guess what he wants.

Though I am not certain my guess is correct, I still open my mouth to speak, full of respect and with my head bowing down. "O, Your Majesty, I come here . . ."

It occurs to me that I've suddenly turned into an actor in some strange theater, and the thought makes me want to laugh and cry at the same time.

"I come here . . . come here . . ."

I repeat myself with some embarrassment, not knowing what reason I should make up. In those wondering moments, I meet the curious gaze of the Princess and then finally I say, "I know that dear King has hung a scroll in search of a prince . . ."

Before I can finish my sentence and before Mr. Tám Tàng has time to answer, the Princess is already waving her hand away. "No, no. I will not select you to be my prince. I chose my prince already."

"Yes, that's true!" Mr. Tám Tàng adds. "I've already selected a prince for my princess."

He lets out a loud scream and his hand lifts the sword over his head.

"You have come here to interfere with me. Your Majesty will not spare you."

He comes bursting out from the doorway while screaming, and I retreat back a few steps, my heart wanting to fall out from my chest.

Mr. Tám Tàng winks at me once more before raising his sword and chopping through the air to lodge the sword into the ground.

My racing pulse recovers a bit when I see him wink at me, but the sword still swishes past my ear and I have to duck then run with all my might.

I hear Mr. Tám Tàng's pounding steps chasing after me, the rustling sounds of his sword's blade swinging through leaves, and his own bellowing voice threatening, "Where to run? When Your Majesty decides to take action, you will have no way out!"

I'm still running like a bat out of hell. At that moment, I still am not sure if his winking is a sign of a conscious man or a crazed man.

74.
Little Nhi

Running so fast that my feet barely touch the ground, I'm panting and my chest is heaving. I only slow down when hearing Mr. Tám Tàng's voice behind me: "Stop, dear boy! I was just pretending."

His voice sounds strange, as if he was borrowing someone else's, and I no longer hear his pounding steps behind me.

When I turn back, Mr. Tám Tàng doesn't look like a king anymore. The crown has fallen off his head somewhere. The scarf is no longer draped around his neck. His hair is frizzy and tangled like dried straw. When I check it more closely I see that the long white shirt has turned an unnameable color, some kind of shade between smoke and grease, and it seems to be made from an old, torn drape. It looks even more rag-gedy and damaged by all the thorns and branches that tore at it while he was chasing after me.

Before me now, Mr. Tám Tàng doesn't look like a king, but he also doesn't look like Mr. Tám Tàng, the pig slaugh-terer who I'd sometimes cross paths with in our village. To my scrutinizing eyes, he appears as just a meager man, hag-gard, as if he's just escaped from a fire. If he's any kind of king, he'd have to be a king whose throne was usurped and who'd had to run for his life for a long time.

"Uncle . . . Uncle . . ." I stammer as I try to take in the man who's now standing so close to me that I can hear his wheezing.

Mr. Tám Tàng sticks his sword into the ground and sighs a long and sorrowful sigh. Only now do I see that his treasured royal sword is simply a wooden one with its grip colorfully painted, like a toy for children.

"My daughter's been a bit touched in the head ever since she fell down at the carnival . . ."

"Little Nhi!" Iquietly gasp.

I know Little Nhi, Mr. Tám Tàng's daughter.

She's the same age as Tường but is one class year behind him in school. Three years ago, a flying motorbike carnival came to our village and set up on our school grounds. Little Nhi was so excited that in the middle of the night, she escaped from her house and went to ask them if she could do the cleaning for the carnival (wanting to see the show every day without having to buy tickets). But her dad, Mr. Tám Tàng, caught her.

Carnivals rarely come through our village as they can't draw the kind of big crowds like in the center of town. That year, the carnival came on account of Uncle Dan asking them so many times. He was acquainted with the leader, who greatly admired his one-handed harmonica playing so much that he often asked my uncle to join the carnival. Uncle Dan always refused with the excuse that he had to look after my grandma.

The flying motorbike carnival brought a motordrome, which was a barrel-shaped cylinder made from wooden planks around ten meters high and set under a canvas tent for shade. The mouth of the barrel had a balcony viewing floor on the outside, also made of wooden planks, and propped up by poles. There was a spiral staircase for the audience to go up to the balcony and watch the show.

The kids in my village were enthralled by the flying motorbike carnival. When the man or woman drove their motorbike out from some secret door to the middle of the empty grounds of the motordrome, giving their engine a loud rev, everyone's heartbeat would quicken.

When the rider drove a few laps on the ground and then suddenly revved their engine and sped up the vertical wall of death, making laps around the motordrome where both they and their bike were parallel to the ground, everyone's heartbeat would nearly burst from their chest.

I still have a clear memory of Little Nhi's accident.

It happened after the day she tried to escape from her father to follow the carnival. She had already been once to see the show, and perhaps out of the fear that she was so obsessed that she'd try to follow them again, her father bit the bullet and got them tickets to see the carnival one more time, to satisfy her craving.

That day, there were two motorbikes riding up on the wall of death at the same time. The man wore a fake beard and a king's clothing, and the woman was in a princess costume. The two motorbikes chased after each other, circling around the motordrome, sometimes darting up, sometimes descending, always spectacular. The King followed behind, sometimes screaming, "Your dear Highness, my Princess, please return to our palace." The Princess genuflected on her motorbike and purred back, "No, I will not, dear Father King."

Us kids were startled so easily, afraid of a collision between the King and the Princess. Only Little Nhi wasn't afraid. Among the so many faces that went pale with fright, she just laughed with delight.

Each time the motorbikes came closer, she would excitedly wave at the King and the Princess. The incident happened as the Princess was playfully driving up higher and higher, her head even peeking up over the mouth of the barrel. She smiled at Little Nhi. No one knows if Little Nhi was incited by some ghost or demon, or if it was just out of excessive excitement, but she stretched her body out from the balcony and reached out to grab the Princess's hand. She gripped that hand for dear life.

I just caught a flash of the performer's frightened eyes and saw her open-mouthed silent scream before she tumbled off the motorbike and took Little Nhi with her. The driverless motorbike kept running another lap around and then flew from the mouth of the motordrome down to the ground as well.

The chaos and fear spread like wildfire across the audience. Screams and shouts turned into a sonic storm that drowned everyone in panic and disbelief.

On the ground, the carnival staff broke out from the hidden side door and bolted over to the two bodies that were lying there, immobile. As if God wanted the tragic event to be even more graphic, when the motorbike came crashing down, it knocked Little Nhi's head. The lightning strike of the ill-fated.

Recalling the incident of that day now, my body still quivers. The images are stitched into my memory, as if someone had sewn this memory inside my head.

In the following days, the performer recovered in hospital with a broken leg and several broken ribs. Only Little Nhi gave us no indication that she'd soon wake up to look at the world once more.

Except for her fragile breathing, her body showed no signs of life. The warmth of her body gradually cooled. The doctors shook their heads. In the end, Mr. Tám Tàng hugged her in sorrow and carried her home, raining tears on his little daughter.

75.
Mr. Tám Tàng's sorrow

Mr. Tám Tàng moved out to Black Cat Hamlet the very next day. He put Little Nhi in an oxcart beside a few meager possessions and silently pulled the cart away before the forlorn eyes watching from behind windows.

He told people he wanted his daughter to be able to rest in a quiet, peaceful space and that there was no way he'd leave her for even just a second.

Mr. Tám Tàng didn't prepare a funeral for Little Nhi, but her death was in our memory because of the way she was lying motionless in the shaky oxcart, moving farther and farther away down the road, through the cemetery, and up the distant Withering Grass Hill, which seemed fixed in the purple light of dusk.

You know, it's even true of the living, let alone the dead. If we don't see them for a long time, they gradually withdraw from us until every last trace of them has vanished from our memories.

Little Nhi not only died, but has been dead for three years. I hadn't thought about her for so long that I almost couldn't imagine there was once such a girl who walked this earth.

Several minutes before, when hearing the Princess call Mr. Tám Tàng "dear King" as he was referring to her as "my dear Highness," it didn't occur to me that there might be some connection between the Princess before my eyes and Little Nhi of days past. Their terms of address, along with their peculiar clothing, were transporting me to some distant land. It wasn't until now, with Mr. Tám Tàng taking off his king's appearance and speaking in ordinary words—"My daughter's been a bit touched in the head ever since she fell down at the carnival"— that I realized the truth.

I am dismayed to learn that Little Nhi isn't dead. Even when rummaging through my mind to recall her face from three years ago, all I can envision is a vague figure. And I know even if I could remember the precise details of Little Nhi's face, the face of a nine-year-old child and the face of an almost-thirteen-year-old girl are surely quite different. I think I still wouldn't be able to recognize her.

Taking into account all of these reasons, neither Tường nor I could have guessed that the mysterious Princess who came to visit our house was the Little Nhi of days before.

I may be rambling, but this movie-like flashback plays out in my head in the few moments before I stammer the question, "So . . . your daughter is . . . still . . . still . . . alive?"

"That's right, she's still alive, dear. I didn't think she'd recover when I brought her here. On that night we moved to Black Cat Hamlet, Mr. Xung came down and took her pulse, opened her mouth, put in a piece of ginseng, packed some medicine . . ."

Mr. Tám Tàng's voice blends with the sounds of the wind and dancing leaves, neither a happy nor sad ensemble. But to hear it makes my heart both uneasy and hopeful.

I direct my eyes toward the branches where sunlight pours in and ask no more questions. Having Mr. Tám Tàng retell a story that he doesn't want to face surely will bring him misery. Though I don't ask, I can still guess the rest of the story: Little Nhi escaped death, but her brain never fully recovered from the impact of the fall and being crushed by the motorbike.

The final image that was imprinted into Little Nhi's mind before she went into a coma was that of a king and a princess. Perhaps for that reason, when she woke up she had the sure belief that she was the Princess and Mr. Tám Tàng was the King, her father.

Little Nhi's cognition is partly disordered, but I can see she's content living in her own land. Mr. Tám Tàng perhaps shares the same idea, and he's been trying to tailor royal clothes for them both and even change their terms of address so his daughter can peacefully live in a dreamy oblivion.

Having to choose this strange way to protect his daughter, I am sure Mr. Tám Tàng's heart aches. Perhaps it's the reason behind the story of a ghost tiger in Black Cat Hamlet as well.

Perhaps Mr. Xung (or someone else) created the story of a ghost tiger so that the kids living by the main road would not dare to venture into Black Cat Hamlet to tease or bother Little Nhi.

Perhaps not every adult in the village is clear about the story from beginning to end, but the ones who do know the hidden truth are surely the confidants of Mr. Xung, helping the father and daughter not have to suffer another unfortunate fate, the fate of people's judgment.

I return home with heavy steps and heavy thoughts. Echoing in my mind is Mr. Tám Tàng's earnest instruction, almost a plea: "Dear boy, if you feel for me, and care for Little Nhi, don't tell anyone the story. Can you do that?"

76.
"I like meeting the Princess anytime, anywhere"

Of course I don't reveal the secret about Mr. Tám Tàng and his daughter to anyone. Except for Tường.

Tường was chosen by the Princess to be her prince; he needs to know who she is. Besides, his magical recovery was very likely set in motion by the Princess's appearance at the window.

"Hey, Tường, I just met the Princess . . ."

When returning from Black Cat Hamlet, I meant to find the least shocking way of beginning the story. But after struggling for a while to find the right words, I just decide to tell him the truth straight away.

Tường doesn't reveal the least bit of surprise. He smiles shyly. "I just met the Princess this morning too."

I take a long breath to calm myself and then continue with the second sentence.

"But I met the Princess where she lives. And I also met her father."

"You met the King too?" Sensing the story is more significant than he previously thought, he raises his eyebrows. "Where is the palace of the King? Is it as beautiful as in the fairy tales?"

I recall the rickety thatched roof of Mr. Tám Tàng and gently shake my head. "Pssh . . . it's a normal house just like ours, that's it."

"The King and the Princess live under a thatched roof, Brother?" Tường nearly shouts out.

I put my hand on Tường's shoulder, as if to be ready to press his shoulder down if he jumps out of his seat from astonishment.

I hesitate. "You know who the King is?" Then I say quickly in one breath, "It's Mr. Tám Tàng the pig slaughterer."

Tường's lips make an A shape. "Mr. Tám Tàng . . ."

"Yeah." I nod my head. "And the Princess is Little Nhi."

Tường immediately remembers Little Nhi. Now his eyes make an O shape. "Little Nhi? Little Nhi died already, Brother."

"She didn't die." I shrug my shoulders. "But now she's become a bit . . . a bit—"

The word "touched" suddenly stops in my throat on its way out. Somehow I don't want Tường to know that part. Little Nhi is his princess and she chose him to be her prince. It's a story that's been nurturing both his body and soul, helping the dreaming tree in his heart to bloom. If he knew his princess was only an insane girl, he'd surely be hurt.

"What is it, Brother?" Seeing me catch myself halfway through my sentence, Tường impatiently urges me on. "Continue about Little Nhi please, Brother!"

I scratch my neck, faltering. "Uhm, I wanted to tell you that now she's a bit . . . a bit . . . not well."

I watch Tường's face as I speak. I'm not afraid that he'll figure out I'm lying, rather, I worry that when he realizes the princess of his heart is in the end just the daughter of Mr. Tám Tàng, the pig slaughterer, he'll feel cheated.

And yet Tường doesn't act like his ship has just sunk. He asks me, with a dreamy voice, "So there isn't a real princess then, Brother?"

"I don't think so." I want to console him. "It's like what I told you the other day!"

"So the Princess is Little Nhi?" Tường exhales. I anxiously watch him as if waiting for a mine to explode, but his next sentence brings me a great relief.

"There was a time when Little Nhi was alive—oh, no, I mean before her accident—that she really liked playing with me. Wherever we went, whatever we did, I was always the person who protected her."

I squint at him. "But she wasn't in the same class as you."

"No, she wasn't, but we still played together." Tường bends his body and points at his feet. "You see this? Look. A scar."

I follow his finger and see a dim scar across his calf.

A hint of a smile slides across Tường's lips but it doesn't

seem like the smile is for me. I get the impression that he's smiling at something that just popped into his head.

"There was one day that Little Nhi was crying like the rain because a bunch of kids were teasing her. As soon as I got there I stepped in."

I lift my eyebrows rather than ask "Then what?"

"I swung my hand at all of them and shouted, 'Let go of her! No one is allowed to bully my friend!' After I yelled they all jumped on me and beat me up. There was one kid with a cane who was wailing against my feet and blood spurt out. To witness that only made Little Nhi cry louder."

"I see." I sniff, feeling bad for not knowing this story before. "Were you ever planning on telling me the history of your scar?"

It seems Tường doesn't want to talk much more about it. He looks out the window and suddenly his tone changes to one of vague sadness.

"So Little Nhi's not doing well, Brother? Poor her."

"Yeah." I answer with just that short word. Actually, I don't know what else to say.

"What illness does she have, Brother?" Tường asks with concern.

I want to make up some reasonable illness but can't come up with one, so I just shake my head. "I'm not sure."

Tường is silent. It seems he's deep in thought as I watch his eyebrows stay furrowed for a while. He abruptly grabs my hands. "Where's her home, Brother?"

I knew sooner or later that Tường would ask this question, but my gut still squirms when hearing it. It's quite difficult for the three words, Black Cat Hamlet, to exit my lips.

"You went to Black Cat Hamlet?" Tường's eyes widen and he doesn't disguise the trembling in his voice when he realizes I met Little Nhi where no one dares to go. "So . . . the ghost tiger—"

181

"I didn't see any ghost tiger at all!" I hastily interrupt his thought. "I'm sure people just made up that story."

Afraid that Tường is going to ask why people would want to make up a story about a ghost tiger, I steer our talk in another direction.

"Do you still feel interested in meeting the Princess after all this?"

Tường responds without thinking, his face as beaming as the afternoon sun. "Of course, Brother. I like meeting the Princess anytime, anywhere."

77.
the Prince's anxious back and forth

Tường still wants to meet the Princess despite knowing that she is just Little Nhi, Mr. Tám Tàng's daughter. It's sweet and surprising.

But many days go by and Little Nhi doesn't reappear as Tường and I lean out the window every day with our eyes expectantly watching Withering Grass Hill.

Tường is now able to walk around the yard, as my my mom watches in radiant satisfaction. He's not yet able to run, but he can walk across the main road to Sister Vinh's house and he can even reach the former house of Little Plum. But I don't encourage him to go any farther, afraid of his exhaustion.

On the fifth day without seeing the Princess, Tường starts to get anxious. He walks around the yard, leans on the fence, stands and fixes his eyes on something somewhere for a bit, then turns back to sit on the bed and opens the storybook about the fire-bellied toad to read. After reading a few pages, he puts the book back down, and drifts back out to the yard.

Watching Tường's anxious back and forth routine, I shake my head. "You're like a busy squirrel, Tường!"

He doesn't reply to this remark, but shows his worry. "I bet Little Nhi got even more sick, Brother."

"No way!" I try to assure him. "Just take it easy, nothing bad has happened to Little Nhi."

The guy Tường seems not to notice my assurances, or if he does notice, he doesn't buy them. With a sentimental look he says, "So why doesn't she visit me anymore?"

"Perhaps she's busy with something else now. When she's not busy anymore, she'll visit you for sure."

I lie. Of course I know why Little Nhi hasn't been back all week. Mr. Tám Tàng is probably keeping an even closer watch over her since the day I unexpectedly turned up at his house and terrified him. Princess Nhi surely misses the Prince Tường, but she can't find a way to sneak back out of her house.

"Or you can bring me to her house so I can visit her?"

Tường's sudden request startles me. I hastily wave away the idea. "No, I can't! Nope, cannot."

"You can, Brother!"

My face becomes serious. "How can you go that far with such legs!"

"I will walk slowly."

Tường looks at me, as if begging, with an intense determination. I sense a fire burning in the depths of his eyes.

"Let me think about it a bit more." I bite my lip, touch my chin, then bite my lip again and hesitate before saying, "Eh, getting over Withering Grass Hill is not a simple task at all!"

"I can climb it!"

Tường is decisive and frank, as if he climbs up the hill several times a day.

Tường's eyes are glued to me. He's on tenterhooks, waiting for my head to nod. I have to face the yard to avoid being swayed.

"Ok! Here it is." A brief pause, and I sigh a long sigh. "I'll take you to Black Cat Hamlet . . ."

"For real, Brother?"

Tường's eyes flash with excitement but immediately dim when I continue, "But not today. You should practice walking for several more days so your legs will be strong enough to make it."

"So tomorrow then, Brother?"

I shake my head. "Tomorrow's not gonna work either."

"So the day after tomorrow," Tường insists. "This afternoon and for the whole of tomorrow I will practice walking, I'll practice until it's too dark to see. Then in the morning after tomorrow, I'll have plenty of energy to walk to Black Cat Hamlet."

I don't think that after only a day and a half Tường will be able to climb up Withering Grass Hill and then cross a sparse forest in Black Cat Hamlet to reach Little Nhi's house. But I don't want to disappoint him so I nod and say, "Yes, if you work hard to practice, I'm sure you'll be able to walk there the day after tomorrow!"

78.
the dragging on days

After eating lunch, as soon as he lays his chopsticks down, Tường stands from his chair and tugs my hand. "Let's go, Brother!"

"Where?"

"You can take me to Mr. Xung's place?"

"Why so far? You're just beginning to practice walking again, you should just go to the First Mr. Hớn's place."

The First Mr. Hớn's house is the former house of Little Plum.

"No, today I'm sure I can walk to Mr. Xung's."

Tường is stubborn, a rare attitude for such a gentle and obedient boy. Perhaps he's got nothing else on his mind except the thought of visiting Little Nhi.

"Your brother's right, dear. It's your first day of practice. Just take a short walk for now and then gradually build it up to be longer." My mom clicks her tongue and gives this advice, of course without knowing the inspiration that's pumping such hopeful anxiety in Tường's heart.

I wink at Tường when seeing his deflated face. "Just listen to Mom!"

That day, Tường actually makes it to Mr. Xung's house. At first, I want to hold his hand and help him along, but he pulls away. "I can do it myself, Brother."

I let go of his hand but do not take my eyes off him for a moment. I only relax a bit when seeing him solidly plant a few slow steps on the ground, as if he were meticulously measuring each foot of the road.

To be honest, when we reach the First Mr. Hớn's house, Tường is just about to collapse. I see his back wet with sweat and raise my voice, worriedly, "Let's go back, kid. We can go walking again tomorrow."

Tường insists, "I'm not tired yet. I can keep walking."

The guy Chair rides his bicycle past, carrying the boy Melon on the back and shouting, "Tường, you can walk again?"

Little Beg sees me and Tường slowly approaching their gate and also comes out. She gives a noisy hurrah. "Hey, Dad! The guy Tường is walking again, come out and see!"

To Tường, the happy astonishment of his friends works like a summer rain bathing the leaves. The tiredness on his face is quickly washed away. I look at Tường, suspecting that he's eagerly threading each of his friend's encouragements into his head. Perhaps he feels like he's climbing Mount Everest!

And Tường's face shines the brightest when Mr. Xung puts a hand on his shoulder and proudly praises him. "You're doing so good, my boy!"

Of course, how could Mr. Xung ever know Tường's hidden motivation to drag himself to their house even before his body was ready. Therefore Mr. Xung is completely ignorant of how his next sentence incidentally paints a sparkling rainbow across Tường's face. "If you keep up this hard practice, in just a few days you'll be running fast as a horse, just wait!"

79.
"the madwoman, the insane one"

Tường is euphoric by the time we get back home from Mr. Xung's house.

I take his hand and ask, "Are you tired?"

"There's absolutely no reason why I should be tired, Brother," Tường answers, intentionally displaying the face of one who thinks walking for such a long time is a piece of cake.

"You're full of it!" I knock him on the head. "Even I got tired, how can you not be?"

Tường gives an embarrassed smile, perhaps realizing he doesn't have to play the hero with me. "Yeah, I'm tired. But just a little bit tired."

He raises his sparkling eyes to look at me. "Tomorrow will you walk with me again then, Brother?"

"Again to Mr. Xung's place?"

"No, tomorrow I want to try to cross the cemetery. I'll go to Withering Grass Hill." As Tường replies this time, his eyes wander from me to an ambiguous place outside the window.

"You are crazed!" I exclaim when learning of his idea. "You couldn't get up that hill!"

"I only want to go to the base of the hill. Then come back."

Tường speaks calmly and yet I can still feel the heat in his words, which he tries to pretend are neutral. I look at him and take a long breath, knowing that I can't and shouldn't prevent him from attaining his desire.

The next morning, after Mom leaves the house, the two of us make our way, step by step, to the cemetery.

But on this day Tường doesn't have enough power to make the whole length of the cemetery. The grass field of the cemetery is bumpy, not smooth like the main road. Tường stumbles many times on the uneven terrain.

This time, not waiting for me to say something first, Tường sits down on the grass, hands rubbing his thighs, and gives his surrender. "Let's go back, Brother!"

"You don't want to practice anymore?" I ask, happily surprised.

"I'll practice again this afternoon," Tường confidently states, wiping the sweat from his forehead.

But something happens that afternoon right when we set foot back at the edge of the cemetery.

It's about four o'clock, the sun not so brutally hot, and on the deep green expanse of the cemetery we glimpse the figures of some kids chasing after each other.

When Tường and I cross the main road, we hear their screams echoing from in front of us.

"What game are they playing, Brother?"

I look at the bunch of kids and shake my head. "Surely just some fighting game."

Tường still squints at the beyond, his legs slowly stepping each step through the late afternoon sun that's shining across the cemetery's iridescent grass.

Suddenly Tường shouts in panic, "Little Nhi, Brother!"

"Little Nhi?" I repeat in amazement.

A deep green dress comes in and out of view among the crowd before us.

It's true, Little Nhi. Why would she appear at this hour? I recall how she has only visited Tường in the mornings or close to noon, when the cemetery is completely deserted.

It's never happened before that Little Nhi escaped in the afternoon. But I only wonder about why for a brief second before it dawns on me. These days, Little Nhi isn't as free to leave Black Cat Hamlet as she was before, so perhaps that's why she has to make a run for it at whatever time her father lets his guard down. She's determined to cross the cemetery at this unusual hour just because she misses Tường so much.

Now the teasing words from the kids chafe our ears more clearly. "The insane girl, hey, guys!"

"The madwoman, the insane one, she goes to seek a husband, the insane one, the madwoman."

While I consider how to sort out my feelings to see what I might do in this unforeseen circumstance, Tường takes off running.

I can't believe my eyes and clumsily start running as hard as I can to follow. Tường falls down once, twice, but he immediately stands back up and keeps running. Tường is not a fast runner, but I am out of breath trying to catch up to him.

When he gets to where the kids are, Tường slaps Melon's hands away as he's grabbing Little Nhi's dress, angrily shouting, "Let go of her! No one is allowed to bully my friend!"

Besides the boy Melon, there are four or five other kids around teasing Little Nhi. When they see the guy Tường's wild eyes flaring like he's ready to kill, the kids fearfully disperse.

Tường stands firmly akimbo and turns around in all four directions, his face burning. "You guys bully someone who's insane and don't feel ashamed, ah?"

So the guy Tường discovers that Little Nhi is mad. My stomach is tense, wondering if he'll be upset, but I'm relieved that he doesn't seem to care about my part in hiding it.

Tường ferociously scans every face in the crowd. "Do you know who this little girl is? It's Little Nhi."

"Who is Little Nhi?" The boy Melon is confused, as if he never knew anyone on this planet named Little Nhi.

I back up Tường's words. "Little Nhi, the daughter of Mr. Tám Tàng."

As if detonating a mine, the kids almost leap from the ground. All mouths agape, they ask, "Little Nhi?"

"How she could be Little Nhi?"

"Little Nhi died already!"

Tường smirks. "Little Nhi didn't die. You got clear proof standing right in front of you. See!"

One kid shouts, "I get it! She didn't die. But she went insane."

At that moment, the kids all glue their eyes to the Princess, who stands there, oblivious. They scrutinize every tiny detail about the Princess, perhaps in an attempt to find some familiar trace to verify that the girl with odd clothes is the same Little Nhi who passed away years ago.

80.

"you're not a prince"

Tường turns back to look at Little Nhi as well. Since he plunged into the crowd and rescued her, the little "princess" has been standing there, motionless, eyes fixed on her "prince."

Tường gets embarrassed when met with Little Nhi's affectionate eyes. With his very slow steps, he approaches the Princess of Black Cat Hamlet.

"Princess, don't be afraid," Tường says, his voice light as a flute's song.

I haven't told him the details of my encounter with Mr. Tám Tàng and his daughter, yet Tường's behavior is no different from mine when I was in Black Cat Hamlet. He doesn't want Little Nhi to be ripped from her private world. Even more, his face and his voice express the fondness and guardianship of a real prince.

Little Nhi slightly nods her head as Tường's speaking.

In response to his friend's gesture, it seems a tiny smile flits across Tường's face. He says with the utmost gentleness, "Dear Princess, do you want to say that you are not afraid?"

Little Nhi again nods her head, and this time her lips quiver. "I'm not a princess."

What Little Nhi utters cannot be more bizarre. I somehow find myself standing beside the two of them without meaning to. The rest of the kids around are also listening to their conversation without the least bit of self control.

Tường frowns a bit. "How do you mean, Princess?"

"I told you, I'm not a princess." Little Nhi repeats her statement purposefully and clearly so that no one could possibly mishear.

Tường points to his chest, perplexed. "So . . ."

"And you're not a prince, either." This time, Little Nhi smiles. "I recognize you now, you are Tường . . ."

If I don't collect myself at this moment, I know I'll fall to the ground.

So it means that Little Nhi is now able to recognize the world. She's left her long delirium in a way that no one was expecting. I pinch my thigh. I'm guessing that a few days ago, when first seeing "Prince" Tường, perhaps she vaguely recognized him, her close friend from the past, in her dim memory. Yet it wasn't until hearing Tường's familiar scream that Little Nhi's mind could be shaken awake.

Standing nearby, the boy Melon and the other kids feel as if invisible hands are choking their throats, so just some mumbling nonsense comes out: "Oh, uhm, she . . ."

This is when the "King" appears.

From the top of the hill, Mr. Tám Tàng comes sprinting down in a huff, his long white shirt soaring behind him, his scarf wrapped around his chest, his wooden sword in hand. Compared to the previous meeting, he is just missing the crown on his head.

I wouldn't have thought that Mr. Tám Tàng was brave enough to cross Withering Grass Hill in such a costume (in truth, I've never seen him in that kind of outfit in the village). But I understand in that moment that when he discovered that Little Nhi was gone, the only concern in his boiling heart was to find his daughter, so he didn't care about changing his clothes.

Spotting Little Nhi surrounded by a crowd, he raises his sword and roars across the distance, "I command you all away from my daughter! If you do not obey, off with your heads!"

Except for me and Tường, none of the kids have any idea of what's going on. The bunch of kids steps backward about ten feet, their faces agitated. The sudden appearance of Mr. Tám Tàng with a sword in hand and violently howling in the wind makes an even more powerful impression than Mr. Four Cang's crazed buffalo scene.

When Mr. Tám Tàng arrives, his face is full of fear. He is waving the sword, his jaw tightly flexed, furiously grinding his teeth. Seeing his daughter at peace, his face relaxes, and though he doesn't say a word, I still can hear some sound gently roaring in his throat.

Surfing his eyes over all of us, he turns to his daughter and says in a hushed voice, "My dear Highness—"

"No, I'm not a Highness."

Mr. Tám Tàng stands his sword on the ground to keep himself from falling over. His face is drained, the crow's feet of his eyes are vibrating: it is now his turn to be bewildered.

"What did you say, my dear Highness?"

"I am Nhi, your child. I am not the child of a king, Dad." Nhi's voice is unbelievably lucid.

"You have called me your dad?" Mr. Tám Tàng innocently asks her and it seems it's he, not his daughter, who's been caught in the world of sleepwalkers.

"Yes. Dad, you are not my king. Dad, you are just my dad," Little Nhi answers while smiling and stepping toward her dad.

The boy Melon is the one who pushes out the words, uttering the thought that's been sprouting in everyone's minds though no one has yet said it: "Little Nhi is awake, Uncle!"

Thanks to his quickness, the smallest boy in the crowd (though he's the same age as Tường and Little Nhi) turns into the messenger of good news today.

81.

I see yellow flowers in the green grass

When a messenger brings good news to kids in a small, poor village such as mine, it means the story no longer has much reason to keep lingering on with you, dear reader.

I would love to say it's possible that Uncle Dan and Sister Vinh will soon come back to the village, as I anxiously await a reunion with the two I have a special love for. The guy Tường perhaps longs for that day even more than me, but if I count Teacher Longan and my grandma, then Tường drops down to third rank.

As for the guy Sơn and Little Three, I have no clue at all, I can't tell their fortune. Perhaps Old Man Huấn and Mr. Four Cang will become in-laws. Perhaps Old Man Huấn will not agree because he looks down on Mr. Four Cang for being so dirt poor, even though Mr. Four Cang is getting richer after making big profits on recent cinnamon trades. Or perhaps it's Mr. Four Cang who will protest the union, denouncing the guy Sơn as ignorant.

Little Plum surely will find her father. And the most beautiful conclusion is that her father, her mother, and she will all return to the village together when they eventually find out that it is not leprosy that her father suffers from, but a certain skin disease. At worst it's psoriasis, which is quite difficult to cure but doesn't force people into isolation.

If Little Plum returns, it's possible my life will be different—surely more mixed up—but whether that means it'll be happier or sadder, I am not so sure. Who knows what "love" can do! But I believe that it will be happier. You know already that if we keep seeing our future through hopeless eyes, how can we survive?

If there's something that gives me idle worry, it's Little Beg's attitude. When I sent the first love letter to Little Beg, she was stupid enough to hand it in to our teacher. But a few months later, she knew to be jealous of Little Plum and refused to take my cinnamon stick gift, which means she's becoming more mature.

Besides these stories, I also hope for my father to have a good job in the city; and I hope the boy Melon, son of Old Mr. Five Bottles, after eating a few more toads will have a growth spurt like the other kids his age so he's not teased as much anymore—though I do enjoy playing around with him for fun.

Oh, perhaps it's too early for me to speak about these things, as actually the story I am telling is still hanging loose here. I recently told the part about the boy Melon announcing that Little Nhi was awake. When he shouted out this news, he put a period on the story of that afternoon. And he nearly put an end to the whole book.

This is because after that, the kids surrounding Little Nhi start to gradually split off. They go toward the pillow trees beside the main road, and huddle up close together to gab away. The melon-like hat of the boy Melon goes up and down in the beehive of heads, like a real melon floating in the afternoon sunlight.

In the opposite direction, Mr. Tám Tàng embraces Little Nhi and slowly walks her back to Withering Grass Hill. In that image of father and daughter, he looks like a real, powerful king who is considerately escorting his princess toward a castle.

Little Nhi takes one or two steps then turns around. I can see the way she affectionately looks back, but anyway, I put my arm around Tường's neck and say, "Let's get home, buddy!"

Tường has no reason not to follow my suggestion. But just like Little Nhi, after a few steps he turns back toward Withering Grass Hill, where his princess seems to walk through the afternoon, only to disappear on the other side of the hill.

I think "Prince" Tường has now repaid his debt to Princess Nhi. If the sudden appearance of the Princess by the window helped the Prince totally forget his hurt back and made him run like a horse, or almost like a horse, then his chivalrous action also incidentally helped the Princess escape the long delirium that had swallowed her life for three years.

While I am aimlessly pondering the magical powers of love—if I could call the strange fondness just blooming in Tường and Little Nhi love (does a princess ever look for a prince to be her husband if not for the sake of love?)—Little Nhi's voice suddenly reaches my ears: "Tường! Wait for me!"

Tường and I abruptly stop for a moment, as if nailed to the grass by Little Nhi's panicked call.

When we jog back, Little Nhi runs up so close to us that we can see some strands of her hair that are sticking to her flushed cheek.

I think Little Nhi will crash right into Tường, who stands there mystified. But she just sets her blue slippers on the green grass, in the proper manner of a lovely and mischievous princess.

I look over, seeing Little Nhi right before Tường's face with just one step between them. Her feet are planted in the grass like two darts, trembling from the sudden stop. The grass underneath her feet is lush but my eyes catch sight of the little petals of a certain yellow flower which blooms discreetly in the shadow of its own leaves. It tells me that the harsh summer will soon pass.

Just standing like that for some moments, Little Nhi raises her sparkling black eyes to watch Tường. She doesn't say a word, but her eyes shine so warmly. When still under the mist of her long fogginess, Little Nhi came by our window to look into the room and catch Tường lying there, immobile on his bed; perhaps she also watched him then as she does now.

It lasts for a while, Little Nhi just standing there looking at Tường, and Tường standing there looking at Little Nhi. The two of them not saying a word, forgetting the hot sun pouring down on their heads, on their shoulders, on their hands, as if without looking at each other, they wouldn't have anything else to do in life.

The King, Mr. Tám Tàng, stands at a distance, with his sword on the ground, looking back toward the Princess and the Prince. I don't know what's going on in his mind.

Before I have time to move, Tường breaks out in a smile.

And at that moment, Little Nhi also smiles. "I'm so thankful for you!" Little Nhi utters this sentence and doesn't look like a princess anymore, though she's still in a princess's costume.

Tường moves his lips up and down when listening to Little Nhi, but in the end he says nothing. I guess he meant to say "I'm so thankful for you too!" but at the last moment perhaps he felt he would just be imitating Little Nhi and decided to keep his silence.

He keeps his silence but his hand grabs Little Nhi's hand.

How innocent he is! Daring to hold Little Nhi's hand in front of her father's eyes. I worry to myself and look over toward Mr. Tám Tàng. However, the cruel "King" is now looking so kind and nice.

Seeing the guy Tường holding his daughter's hand slightly startles him and he lifts his sword. But he doesn't say, "I command you all away from my daughter! If you do not obey, off with your heads!" this time.

He simply lifts the sword to scratch his calf. Perhaps there's an insect biting him . . .

About the Author

Nguyễn Nhật Ánh grew up in Quảng Nam province of central Vietnam and started writing stories and poems at the age of 13. To this day, he has written more than 100 titles, which put him in Vietnam's *Guinness Book of Records* in 2005 as the most prolific author for children and young adults, though his writings have been warmly embraced by readers of all ages.

Among some of the author's many achievements, Nguyễn Nhật Ánh earned the Southeast Asian Writers' Award in 2010 and has been recognized with awards from the Vietnamese Writers' Association (2003, 2009) and the Vietnamese Publishers' Association (2009). Nguyễn Nhật Ánh's books were bestsellers at Ho Chi Minh City's international book fair on three separate occasions (2008, 2010, 2016), while the original Vietnamese versions of such titles as *Kính Vạn Hoa* (*Kaleidoscope*) and *Cho tôi xin một vé đi tuổi thơ* (*Ticket to Childhood*) were included on a list of "105 Most-Read Books of the World" that Ten Books Publishing House in Japan compiled in 2013. His books *Tôi là Bêtô* (*I am Bêtô*) and *Cho tôi xin một vé đi tuổi thơ* (*Ticket to Childhood*) were also voted to the "Most-Beloved Books" list by readers of *Người Lao Động* journal in 2007 and 2008.

Rex
Fred Yager
Available in e-book, print, and audiobook versions

Davy Ross is back in Manhattan with his grandmother when he learns that his parents, paleontologists, are missing in Africa. A trunk soon arrives and Davy finds an egg in it. He sets it on a shelf and during the night, it hatches. As the story unfolds, readers witness the friendship of a young boy raising a creature long believed to be extinct as he tries to solve the mystery of his parents' fate.

REVIEWS:

"In *Rex*, by Fred Yager (co-author of *Untimely Death*), 11-year-old Davy Ross's paleontologist parents go missing from a dig on Mount Kilimanjaro, and he finds a mysterious egg among their belongings. When a tiny dinosaur hatches, Davy has to protect him from an unscrupulous professor, return the tyrannosaurus to its jungle home and locate his missing parents."—*Publishers Weekly*

"The author, a screenwriter, has presented a very visual story that's fast-paced and full of action...."

—*School Library Journal*

Doodles Lanhorn and the Great China Adventure
Russell D. Bernstein
2021

Take a journey into the magical, creative world of Doodles Lanhorn, a fourteen-year-old boy gifted with exceptional Wizartry powers, where the art of drawing makes something come to life just with the whirl of his hand! In this latest adventure, Doodles takes an action-packed trip to China to compete in the annual Wizartry Competition, determined to win a seat on the Wizartry Council even though he is the youngest contestant, so he could change the realm for the better. But Doodles must face old and new enemies, somehow manage to win the competition against all odds, if he is to save Wizartry from the powerful forces that are trying to take over the enchanted world. This is the fourth book in the Doodles Lanhorn series, including the second novel, Doodles Lanhorn and the Quest to Save Inner Earth, which was an Amazon bestseller when it was published in 2016. Although Russell D. Bernstein's latest Doodles novel, *Doodles Lanhorn and the Great China Adventure*, stands alone although Doodles Lanhorn fans of all ages may want to read all the novels in the series.

Advance quote:
"An inspiring, creative, Harry Potteresque novel for coming-of-age teens. *Doodles Lanhorn and the Great China Adventure* will not only entertain young readers, but it will expand their imaginations through its effortless and thrilling story line."
—Ashley Hazan

Doodles Lanhorn and the Quest to Save Inner Earth

Russell D. Bernstein

2016 (134 pages)

Available in e-book, print, and audiobook versions

Doodles Lanhorn is a red-headed boy of thirteen who doesn't feel very popular or successful but he does have a special talent: he has recently discovered the powers of Wizartry, the art of drawing something and making it come to life. Doodles comes to learn that he is unique in that he does not require a paintbrush like most Wizarts; he can draw with just the use of his hands. In this new novel, Doodles must deal with old enemies, rescue his family, and ultimately save Inner Earth, the sacred land of the Wizarts. With the help of his friends Laura, Darren, and Boogley, a very unique and special creature, Doodles is able to overcome his fears so he can face all these obstacles, head on.

PRAISE:

"*Doodles Lanhorn and the Quest to Save Inner Earth* is a great read...."

—C.J., 12-year-old seventh grader

"A modern-day fable of an innovative boy using his creativity to develop strategies to successfully defeat bullying."

—Paula Fradiani, Ed.D., child advocate

Doodles Lanhorn and the Search for the Missing Artifact
Russell D. Bernstein
2017 (142 pages)
Available in e-book, print, and audiobook versions

Art comes to life as Doodles uses his exceptional Wizartry skill to hunt for the prized artifact that holds the key to Inner Earth. But there is a detective who is convinced that Doodles is the actual thief. Doodles enlists the help of his old and new friends, including his unique sidekick Boogley. Will Doodles recover the stolen artifact or will the malicious Mr. Derringer outwit him? Although this new novel is a standalone book, Bernstein is also the well-regarded author of *Doodles Lanhorn and the Quest to Save Inner Earth*, among other novels.

PRAISE:
"A perfect read for any young adult who has questioned whether they fit in and who they can trust in their own life."
—Kate Singley, 6th grade teacher

"Doodles Lanhorn and the Search for the Missing Artifact is a truly enjoyable story. I liked how Doodles grew and developed, while simultaneously trying to prove himself as a Wizart AND trying to recover the artifact, all while struggling through eighth grade. I will definitely recommend this book to my peers."
—C.J., 8th grader